GW01046895

PHRASE SEVEN

By CHASE HUGHES

"One man who can persuade a country's leader is more powerful than their entire military infrastructure."

- Alex Frost, former director of HIG

Dedicated to the faceless ghost soldier of the Yorktown Victory Monument.

The man who stands at gates of peace
will never be known to any.
His words, the swords that he'd release
in the name and spirit of many.

To guard their lives, I stand here now
to watch over sea and land
to persuade for peace, my solemn vow
in the mind, I make my stand.

These words I know and keep in shroud
shall never see the light
till country's call and kings have bowed
and peace has more the might.

History will come to show
what most will surely find,
the start and end of what we know
begins within the mind.

Editing: Deserae Hunter, Stephanie Cook, Sasha Leongson, Polly Cassandra, Jessica Scurlock, Bethany Votaw, Anna Read

Cover art: Paul Campbell

ISBN: 978-0-578-64285-7

Some physical locations may exist. Google away.

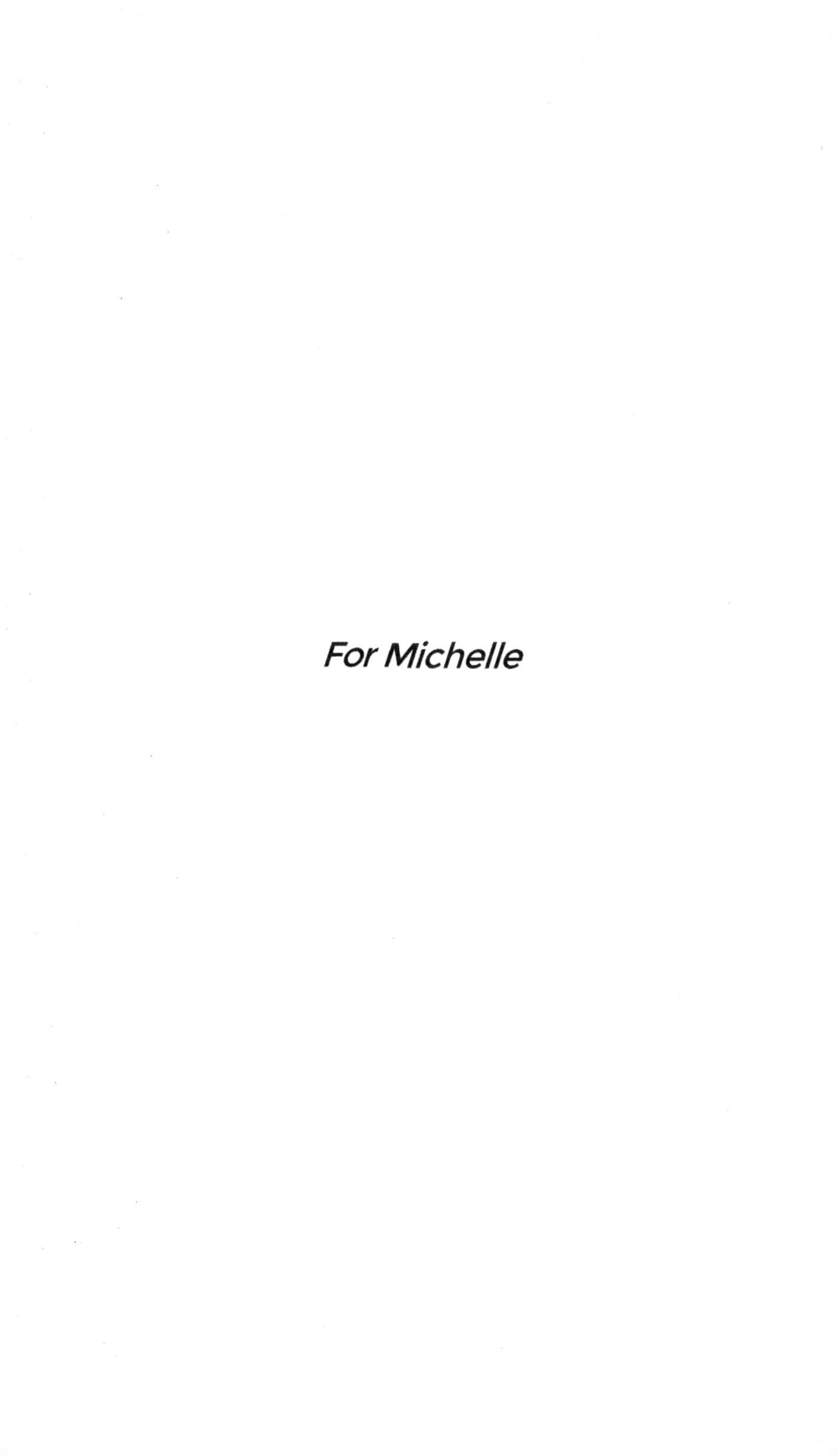

For Michelle

CONTENTS

PROLOGUE SAN JOSE, CALIFORNIA

When the man spoke, she became a hollow puppet and the part of her that could resist vanished.

"I'll be very upset if you vomit in this car. Big girls don't do that."

It was dark outside, and occasional neighborhood lamp posts crept past the windows of the long black BMW. The car rode quietly as gravel crackled under the tires. Nicole looked at the bearded man sitting beside her in the backseat, a thirty-something who looked like a military guy. His beard pushed on the collar of his flannel shirt.

Nicole heard herself saying, "No... they don't."

Why am I agreeing with him?

She blinked heavy eyes at the bearded man beside her, squinting to bring his features into focus. It was no use; the dense white fog that had been clouding the edges of her vision for the last day wouldn't disperse. Her mind sagged under the weight of that fog, and it was an effort to stay conscious. This man had done this to her somehow, and she had become used to it over the last twenty-four hours. She had never killed anyone until twenty minutes ago, and the man with the beard had told her to '*feel just fine*' with it. She didn't feel much of anything at all, but somewhere inside of her, there was disagreement - like in her belly. It wanted out.

She tried to focus elsewhere. She thought of her family, her yoga studio, her student debt. It was no use. The seat smelled like rich leather and bourbon. She leaned her head against it, hoping the smell could help keep her mind off everything. The Beard Man watched her. His gaze seemed paternal.

I feel like a child inside - he's enjoying it.

The staccato click of the BMW's turn signal sent her attention forward to an unfamiliar neighborhood appearing in the windshield.

"We're almost there," said the older man behind the wheel. The driver wore a sharp suit that reminded her of her dad.

The Beard Man took in a slow, calm breath.

His breathing is perfect for yoga.

He leaned forward and grabbed the side of the driver's seat. "Make yourself safe now, Mike."

She turned her head to see the driver pulling at a wire from somewhere beside him. He fumbled with it for a bit, produced a set of earbuds, and pressed them deep into his ears. Jazz music blasted from the tiny speakers. The driver reached beside him again and found a set of hearing protection earmuffs, like the construction workers behind her yoga studio wore. He steered with his knee while he pulled them onto his head, pushing them against his ears. He then grabbed the wheel, lifted his hand, and shot a 'thumbs up' gesture to the Beard Man.

The Beard Man patted the driver on the shoulder, then turned back to Nicole. He sat back in his seat and looked her body over, and his lips squeezed together in what seemed like shame – maybe regret.

"Nicole, you're so gorgeous, and you did a great job tonight. Are you ready for this to be over?"

Her face was still resting against the seat, but she felt herself nodding.

A second later, there was a hand on her shoulder, and the Beard Man spoke a word in a deep voice that sent ice-cold electricity down her spine.

"Listen..."

She knew he was saying *that phrase* again. She heard the second word, 'Nicole' and felt a forceful wave of gravity pull her into the seat. She heard the echo of a few more words she was never quite able to distinguish. Part of her mind went somewhere else. The part of her that stayed with this man would do things she didn't like.

She had only known him for a day. Her life was ruined. *She* was ruined.

All because she had raised her hand at dinner, twenty-eight hours ago.

CHAPTER 1

PRAGUE, CZECH REPUBLIC

Pierce Reston waited in the dark behind a small crop of trees for the man who would arrive soon. The cool night air blew through the wooded area, sending the smell of damp moss through the small forest surrounded by the bustle of Prague.

Human trafficking had been on the rise in Prague, and over the last month, eleven American girls had been reported missing. Pierce needed answers, so he had tracked down Ivan Markov, the man responsible for the three-hundred-million-dollar enterprise in Prague. Over the previous two days, Pierce had watched him patiently. His home was on a narrow backstreet abutting a wooded park. A few neighbors, but far enough away that he was able to live a relatively private life. With the woods so close to the house, Pierce had no trouble observing the man's habits from cover.

Ivan left every day to run the trails in the wooded Košíře-Motol park. The man would leave through his garage, cross under the railroad tracks behind his home, and enter a running trail at around 3:10 every morning. He was a maniac—up around three every day, and in bed before eight every night. This early in the morning, Pierce assumed, Ivan Markov ensured no one else would be on the trails to disturb him. Or see him. Pierce assumed the man had only recently begun to run every morning, as Ivan looked slightly overweight.

This was a perfect location to take him down. His family, who Pierce didn't want to disturb, was in the house, and if he got the man while he was out of breath on a run, his brain would be far more likely to default to *surrender* instead of *fight*.

Pierce had been able to track the man down using a set of credentials that identified him as a US State Department official. The Czech police had been helpful, and his sharp jawline and short dark hair helped him blend in with the locals as he traveled the city hunting Ivan.

Ivan had made his millions kidnapping, selling, and shipping young women to the highest bidder. The asshole had spent a lifetime in Prague, building an empire by networking into elite circles and making massive donations to local politicians.

Pierce had rigged a fourteen-foot-long wire to a tree across the running trail from him. With the cable laid across the jogging path on the dirt, he sat on the other side, holding the end of the wire in his hand. He glanced down at the glowing hands of his Seiko. By his estimate, the man would come around the corner in about three minutes.

Keeping his eyes on the trail, he lifted a water bottle next to his *Code of Bell* sling bag filled with cold vodka and took a sip.

To his left, the rhythmic scuff of footsteps on the trail grew clearer. He tightened his grip on the wire and shifted onto a knee.

The footsteps drew closer. He made out the outline of a slightly overweight man about 20 yards from him jogging down the path. He was alone. The man's cell phone flashlight shined through the pocket of his gym shorts as he rounded the corner, heaving, quick breaths as his feet thudded on the trail.

Pierce waited for the man to reach the wire and jerked it tight with both hands, throwing the weight of his body behind it.

The wire tightened and almost pulled Pierce off his feet as the heavy man's knees collided with the obstacle. His body flew forward and skidded into the earth with force that vibrated under Pierce's feet. A deep, loud cough erupted from the man as his chest slapped against the earth.

Pierce spun, grabbed the wire in his left hand, and drew his Glock pistol with his right. He was on the man in an instant. Pierce wrapped the wire twice around the man's neck and lifted the man's sweating face to the barrel of his gun before the man even realized how he'd fallen.

"Ivan Markov?" Pierce asked in a pleasant voice.

The man's eyes grew as he looked at Pierce. His expression flashed from shock to anger.

Pierce hauled the man to his knees by the wire and knelt in front of him, keeping a firm grip on the wire wrapped around the man's neck.

"Ivan Markov?" Pierce repeated.

"You're making the biggest mistake of your life," Markov seethed between rapid breaths.

Pierce smiled. "I'll be the judge of that. Besides, you won't remember this conversation at all. Your English is excellent, by the way."

In one swift motion, Pierce holstered his Glock and withdrew a small syringe from his back pocket. He pulled the man upward by the wire, buried the needle into his neck, and emptied its contents.

"What the hell is this?"

"It's called Sodium Amytal," Pierce replied in a matter-of-fact tone.

"I'll kill you," the man spat as his body sagged into the ground below.

"Relax. You won't even know this happened."

Sodium Amytal was one of the more common 'truth serums' in the world. Classified as a 'hypnotic' drug, it created a mental state of complete surrender and compliance. In the right dose, it would help to erase any memories Pierce couldn't delete using hypnosis techniques alone.

After a minute, Ivan's breathing slowed, and his body relaxed into a seated position on the trail.

"Listen, Ivan. I only need some information. You like kidnapping girls. You're the local expert. I've got some missing girls from the US I need help finding."

Ivan exhaled a small giggle under his breath. The man was turning into a carefree, sweaty idiot.

"No one kidnaps Americans here. It's the stupidest thing you can do. Your State Department would cause too many problems."

"Are you being honest with me, Ivan? It's really important for your family's safety that you're honest with me. Tell me where the American girls are."

He saw a small flash of anger on Ivan's face at the mention of his family. Pierce had no intention of hurting them, but the threat was usually enough to bring a person's stress level to the point where they would reveal more behavioral cues of deception. The man was telling the truth.

"Ivan, look at me."

Ivan's eyes drifted up to Pierce.

"I need to know where the girls are. If you didn't take them, I need you to find out who did. Here's what's going to happen: you're going to listen to my voice. The more you listen to this voice, the more your mind can focus, becoming even more relaxed with each one of those breaths..."

Pierce didn't use hypnosis often, as it wasn't a useful tool in the field unless you injected the person first. The injection really helped with compliance.

The man nodded, his head lolling to one side. His gaze and his mind were a thousand miles away.

Pierce picked up Ivan's hand and slid the man's phone into it.

"Unlock your phone and send a text to all of your people."

The man unlocked his phone and clumsily opened a messenger app.

"Ivan, do you have a group chat where you can send a message to everyone?"

"Y—yes. Secure encrypted group. Here."

He pointed to a group of contacts called 'Nouzové / Všichni.' *Emergency / All.* The group contained 291 contacts.

"Great. That's great, Ivan. Click on that one, and you will type the message you will hear from me."

Ivan nodded, tapping on the group.

Pierce narrated his message slowly, keeping an eye on the trail. "Compromised. Shut down operations and destroy all electronics. Release all girls immediately with their papers."

Pierce helped him send the message and used one final technique to ensure amnesia would take hold, even if the injection couldn't expunge the whole memory.

"You're going to discover how easy it is to *forget all of this.* Like scratches on a CD, or wiping off a chalkboard and simply erasing this moment.

Everything in your mind removes every detail of what *didn't* happen here. Like little bacteria in your brain, right there in your brain now, eating, destroying, eliminating, and removing every single detail from this event. Every time you stand from a seated position, this command will reactivate, deleting everything. You're on a good morning run, you're safe."

Pierce hauled the sweating man upright and walked him back to the trail, where he told him to keep jogging.

*****

A thundering knock on his hotel room door shook Pierce from his sleep. He instinctively grabbed the cold grip of his Glock under the adjacent pillow and tried to orient himself. Pierce squinted at the bedside clock. 6:04 AM. He had only been back from the woods for two hours.

The forceful knocks continued, echoing in the cold, cramped room.

"Mister Thomas?" a shout echoed from the hallway.

He'd been using the cover name Greg Thomas in Prague while speaking with the local police about the missing women. After viewing all the evidence the police had about the missing girls, everything indicated that the girls really did disappear when they arrived at the airport.

Pierce navigated his way through the small room to the light switch near the cheap wooden door.

"Who's there?" he asked through the decaying wood.

"Police, sir."

Pierce slid the Glock into a stack of towels and unchained the door. He cracked it open to see two uniformed police officers in the hallway.

"Mister Thomas. Inspector Andera needs to speak with you, sir. We can wait while you get dressed."

Pierce had spent the previous day working through all the police files on the missing girls with Inspector Andera. Human trafficking was bad in Prague but taking American girls from an airport was *not* what those people did.

"It's six in the morning, guys. What's going on?"

"I'm afraid it's urgent, Mister Thomas. Please hurry."

"I'll be right out," Pierce said.

Pierce threw on a clean black suit and white dress shirt in front of the mirror. Despite his dark brown hair and athletic physique, his tanned skin had alerted everyone in Prague he wasn't a local. Everyone he spoke to somehow knew he was American, defaulting to speaking English before he could utter a word. He splashed cold water onto his face and decided not to shave.

Pierce exited and an officer handed him a cup of coffee. He descended three floors in silence with the two armed officers. After a short drive on Prague's empty streets, the officers stopped in front of a stone four-story hotel. Spotlights sent light crawling up the tall exterior walls, and layers of stone towered into castle-like archways and terrace railings above.

"Hotel Carlo the Fourth," one of the officers said. "Inspector Andera is waiting on the roof, sir."

Pierce felt a disquieting sense of curiosity about meeting the detective on a roof. To the left of the hotel entrance, a string of police tape encircled an area full of officers. Through the window of the police vehicle, sporadic camera flashes illuminated the area.

Pierce's car door opened. The young officer extended a guiding hand to the front door of the ominous hotel.

Pierce exited the police car and walked with one officer to the uninhabited lobby.

"During the communist regime, this hotel was the headquarters of the Czechoslovakian Postal Service," the officer said as they entered the lobby.

Pierce's gaze was met by two lone hotel employees clad in black suits at an antique reception desk. His eyes drifted downward to the pristine, polished marble floors. Ornate columns and rows of intricate design climbed the tall white walls to the pearly ceiling above. They neared the elevator, footsteps echoing off the vacant floors in the lobby.

This would put rooms in the Sistine Chapel to shame.

As the doors to the white marble elevator glided shut, the officer removed his hat and turned to Pierce.

"Sir, we've found one of your American girls. No one can explain what happened."

PHRASE SEVEN

CHAPTER 2
PRAGUE, CZECH REPUBLIC

"She just got naked and walked off the roof of the hotel. She was very happy, sir," a weathered Detective Andera spoke in broken English and withdrew a cigarette from a crumpled pack as he spoke to Pierce.

A pile of discarded women's clothing lay nearby on the roof. The gentle morning breeze brought the sleeve of a blouse into motion. A pile of something only the living deemed important.

Pierce knew the answer, but still asked, "You think she walked off by accident?"

"No, sir." The detective lit a cigarette and exhaled a narrow stream of smoke at his feet. "She posted a live video, sir. The Internets." He dug into his coat pocket, produced a mobile phone, and tapped the screen a few times.

"They took the video down, but the police have it on a server."

Pierce's stomach sank. He took the phone from the detective's outstretched hand, blew the stray cigarette ashes from the screen, and played the video. He watched a young and beautiful girl aim the camera at herself on the rooftop where he now stood. She focused her attention on someone just behind the camera, nodded her head, and turned back to the camera with a smile.

"Okay. I've been asked to take off my clothing and walk off the roof," she said lightly, her smile dazzling.

The camera shook as she pulled at her garments one-handed. Pierce watched closely for any fluctuation in her expression. Surprisingly, undressing in public while streaming live video caused the girl no discernible insecurity. She seemed calm—centered. The skin under her eyelids was wrinkle-free, and her pupils dilated as she looked at whoever was speaking to her.

Completely naked, she walked up the wet incline of the red tiles of the roof, and down the short decline opposite to the edge.

She's still smiling.

The woman came to a knee-high stone railing, sat on it, and swung her legs over. There, at the top of the hotel, she looked down upon the nighttime bustle in the streets of Prague. She looked into the camera, smiled, and spoke her final words:

"Guys, let's go down to the street. The *front* of this building is *so* gorgeous at night."

The woman casually stepped off the roof. Pierce's jaw clenched. He fought to control his breathing in front of the detective. He had always feared an event like this could occur.

He peered down at the stone street and watched the crowd around the body. A sheet now covered the young woman. Three policemen shielded her body with umbrellas from onlookers taking photos of the scene.

Pierce typed out a quick, secure message to HIG headquarters:

Confirm one dead. Possible Enhanced Persuasion victim.

Within seconds, a return message from the HIG Director, Deidra Collins, came back.

Copy. Need you back in Virginia first thing tomorrow. Emergent.

Pierce Reston had seen two very distinct things in this video that he had hoped never to see. Those eyes, and the muscles around them, had revealed his single greatest fear: an outbreak no medicine on earth could cure.

CHAPTER 3

YORKTOWN, VIRGINIA

"In just a moment, we'll walk through how to talk someone into robbing a bank."

Kelly Kennedy sat at her dark wooden desk with the other students in the small, luxurious classroom surrounded by oil paintings of men and women they weren't privileged to know about, yet. It always smelled like old books. Kelly kicked off her shoes and let her feet rest on the soft, green carpet.

Alex Frost, the lead instructor and former director of HIG, addressed the small class of five students who had spent almost the entire year in training. Alex, with short gray hair and an athletic frame, now in his seventies, was an icon at HIG.

Alex continued, "When you joined HIG, you signed more non-disclosure agreements and binding contracts than you've ever thought possible. Since it is Friday on your final week of training, I'll share a few things with you before you graduate on Monday.

"We've kept so much information from you because this year hasn't just been training. It's been a test. We wanted to verify you'd keep the techniques to yourself and the identity of HIG a secret. You'll learn a lot about HIG next week after you graduate, *including* what HIG stands for. Students are forbidden to know what it stands for until their graduation for a *very* good reason; it speaks to our origins.

"When you were all recruited, you were approached by someone from the State Department who told you that you have been admitted into a secret organization. We are *not* the State Department. HIG is not officially part of the government. We work *with* the government, and the government works with us, but we are beholden to no one except HIG staff. We are our own entity. An agency, but not a government one. We've invested around eight million dollars in each of your trainings this year, and your sleepless nights have paid off. You're all about to learn the real history of HIG, and you'll realize why we don't discuss it until graduation."

Kelly shot a hand into the air and said, "How does the government allow us to operate?"

"We have a hall pass from the Founding Fathers with no expiration date. It's also why we're in Yorktown. Now, back to the bank robbery..."

The students exchanged open-mouthed glances.

Kelly had been recruited into the most secretive organization in America and, with only a day left of training, had never heard her instructors, especially Alex, talk about robbing banks...or, for that matter, the Founding Fathers.

"Getting someone to rob a bank is the same as talking someone into spying, disclosing secrets, telling you the location of chemical weapons, or revealing vital intelligence. What do these all have in common?"

A student next to Kelly raised a hand and the instructor nodded.

"They aren't necessarily in someone's best interest?"

"Perfect. Right," Alex continued. "So, how would you have someone rob a bank? *Basic* hypnotists have done it. Even during my childhood, it was being researched. Orne, Estabrooks, and Evans were some of the lead researchers in making people commit crimes, even murder, under hypnosis."

"To rob a bank, I'd want to have someone suggestible," another student spoke up to Kelly's left.

The instructor nodded. "We can modify suggestibility—make someone more suggestible. You all have endured combat training, intelligence work, counterintelligence training, and the most elite persuasion and influence training in the world. You can't convince someone to rob a bank?"

The five students sat in silence.

Kelly sat upright. "I think...we are all wondering if this is some test," she said, smiling.

Alex smiled. "This entire year has been a test of integrity. Even learning what HIG *stands for* is a privilege. I am, however, exploring how you all would do this with limited time. You can answer. No test. I promise."

Amused, Kelly clicked her pen while she ran through several scenarios in her head. "I wouldn't use hypnosis. Takes too long. But you'd still have to select someone who was highly suggestible if you only had a couple minutes."

Alex nodded for her to continue.

"I'd use confusion initially. And follow up with joint touching, name usage, and then use commands to bypass their defenses and send their ass into the bank."

Alex raised an eyebrow and grinned. "Okay, Ms. Kennedy. Care to explain your thought process?"

Kelly leaned forward, elbows on her desk. "Confusion works in the brain the same way that thinking we're drowning makes our arms and legs flail around. When a person is drowning, they will immediately grab onto any object they touch, even if it's a hot poker or a thorn bush. When someone hears something that confuses their mind, they will automatically accept the first *logical* thing they hear to lessen the confusion.

"I would use a standard confusion statement and immediately follow that with their name. A person's name brings immediate attention to the moment, gets them prepared for the suggestion—in this case, to rob the bank. I'd touch them on a joint as I said their name. Contact with joints causes a mammalian response. All animals' joints are vulnerable, and it creates a lot more awareness when someone touches a joint versus when someone just touches an arm or something. I'd touch him on the wrist or elbow while speaking his name, then use, like, two or three hidden commands to compromise his judgment and bypass his willpower."

The instructor nodded. "Great job, Kelly. If you were able to profile this person, you'd also be able to use their fears, and the words you know will trigger this person on an *individual* level. You all know how to profile, and this would be the one time to use all the behavioral information in a single sitting."

"What would that sound like?" Alex's deep, raspy voice reminded her of her grandfather.

Kelly thought for only a moment before she launched into her demonstration.

"I'm certain how different would it be if the same things started looking now like it wouldn't change if nothing else really did? And it's easy to just ***let go, now, with me***, I think it's amazing how little real control we have. And a lot of us have this voice," Kelly pointed to her mouth, "that's able to completely guide you. Some people get into trouble when they don't ***listen closely to this voice and do what it says*** to them. And it would be easy to just let the thoughts you notice coming in about the bank here in your mind," she pronounced the phrase "your mind" as **you're mine**. "They have no issue with you going in letting them know you're going to set off a bomb unless they ***fill a bag with money for you***–to be confident, as you may notice happening now–is the time to really think about taking action–is what's really required with this–is something you can ***easily do–this now*** as you go on into the bank here."

Kelly had been taught to hide words in her speech. She'd discovered early in HIG training how easy it was to make the subconscious hear something as a completely separate command, where the conscious mind was given no opportunity to scrutinize the phrase or decide if it was in their best interest. In the middle of a sentence, Kelly could place a 'command' hidden in her language only heard by the unconscious. All she'd learned to do was pause briefly before and after the statement and lower her voice slightly as she spoke the hidden words. The first time she used them on a person for her HIG homework, she was in awe of the power it possessed.

Any human could be hacked into and modified.

CHAPTER 4
PRAGUE, CZECH REPUBLIC

The morning sun climbed over Prague. Pierce pulled up his collar against the breeze and clicked the magnetic locking mechanism on his sling bag across his body. He eyed the line of cars cluttered the street across from the hotel that was now a crime scene. Most of them were unoccupied police vehicles, lights still flashing. One vehicle, however, captured his attention. A small, black Skoda sedan at the back of the line, thirty yards to Pierce's right.

Inside the Skoda, a man sat and watched in complete stillness. Pierce held his phone closer to his face, so it looked like he was checking his phone instead of eyeing the man.

He edged along the sidewalk in front of the hotel, keeping a close eye on the sedan. With it parked across the street in the back of the line of vehicles, there was little chance he could get the man by surprise.

He passed the line of cars and slipped across the cobblestone street fifteen yards behind the Skoda. In one hand, Pierce held his State Department credentials, the other gripped firmly on the Glock in his waistband. As he neared the vehicle, Pierce softened his steps to look more casual.

He eyed the man's face in the side mirror and came within a foot of the vehicle when the man's head snapped left to see Pierce approaching. His eyes widened at the sight of Pierce, and in a flurry of movement inside the car, the engine roared to life. Tires screamed on the slick rock as the small sedan sped off around a corner.

Pierce sprinted forward to the nearest police BMW and yanked the handle to find it unlocked. He leapt into the still-running vehicle, pulled it into drive and slammed the accelerator down to the floor. Shouts erupted from the crowd of nearby police as he spun the wheel to the right after the fleeing vehicle.

Just ahead, Pierce found his target. The black sedan sped down Senovážné náměstí and took a sharp right and then a sharp left onto náměstí Republiky. The minimal traffic gave way to Pierce, allowing him to close in on the speeding Skoda.

The police BMW grabbed onto the centuries-old roads of Prague, and its bumpy nature bounced the underside of the car against the bricks as Pierce sped after the fleeing vehicle. The man led him through a maze of turns and skidded past a group of tourists in a crosswalk who were blindly following a tour guide carrying a large blue umbrella. Pierce jerked the car onto the sidewalk to avoid them. A trail of police lights appeared in his rearview mirror. His heart thundered as he gained on the fleeing man.

The man spun the sedan hard to the left down a narrow road. The tires screeched again on the uneven brick as the BMW dropped off the sidewalk and he turned right onto Husova. Only fifty yards behind the sedan, Pierce kept the accelerator mashed into the floor.

The man turned the wrong way onto a narrow, one-way street. A hundred yards ahead, a large delivery truck whipped out from behind a parked Volkswagen, blocking the road in front of them. Pierce again slammed the gas pedal down and leaned back to avoid the soon-to-explode airbag. The BMW's engine screamed as Pierce smashed into the rear of the Skoda, sending it hurling forward. The impact slammed the Skoda into the delivery truck.

Pierce wrenched the police vehicle into park and jumped out. The man leaped from the broken, steaming car and shot a glance at Pierce. He was lanky, Middle Eastern, and dressed in a non-descript black jacket and ball cap. He turned back to the narrow road as a large, angry man screamed in Czech from the window of the delivery truck. Pierce bounded over the crumpled hood and went at a full sprint after his target.

The tall man ran past the Apple Museum of Prague and took an immediate right into an alley of shops that had yet to open. Pierce followed with controlled breathing and laser focus. The man snaked through the street and veered right toward Prague's Old Town Square. Only a hundred feet in front of Pierce, the man dug into his rear pocket as he ran. His furious digging slowed him down, allowing Pierce to close distance.

The man produced something from his pocket, tilted his head back, and shoved the object into his mouth. He sprinted past the Astronomical Clock Tower and turned toward the center of the stone square. He glanced back as Pierce came closer. Their footsteps echoed in the empty square, and he could now hear the man's heaving breaths up ahead.

The man glanced back again at Pierce, shoving yet another object into his mouth. Now within arm's reach, as they neared the center of the square, Pierce shoved the man forward with all of his weight. The man stumbled forward and tripped over the chain surrounding the Jan Hus Memorial statue in the center of the Old Town Square.

The man's forehead cracked against the gray stone steps at the base of the mammoth monument, and his groan echoed across the square. He clumsily pulled himself up to a seated position, his back against the memorial. Pierce stepped over the chain and knelt beside the man. Blood streaked his face. Before Pierce could say a word, thick, white foam oozed from the man's mouth. His eyes turned a bright red and his body went into rapid convulsions for only a second before he collapsed into a lifeless form.

"Fuck," Pierce exhaled.

Still breathing heavily, Pierce gazed up at the Jan Hus Memorial, commemorating the martyrdom of Jan Hus, who died willingly to stand in opposition to the invasive persuasion of the Vatican in Prague.

Pierce spun to see a fleet of police rounding the corner of the Astronomical Clock. Inspector Andera pulled into the square behind Pierce in a police SUV and flew out of the vehicle toward him, his eyebrows clenched in anger.

He marched over to Pierce. "What the hell is this? You steal a police car?"

Pierce held his hands up in surrender. "Inspector, this man was watching the scene at the hotel; I think he's involved with the missing girls. I know I have diplomatic immunity, but I should not have done that. I am very sorry."

"Where is he?" The detective's eyebrows shot up with excitement.

"He's at the base of the statue. He took some kind of suicide pill," Pierce said, still attempting to catch his breath.

The detective held up a hand and yelled to his men, "Don't touch the fucking body. No one approach the body! Get the tourists out of here, now."

"Detective, I'll be right back. I have to make a call."

Andera eyed him. "I will send an officer with you. You may not be safe here."

Pierce knew Andera was sending an officer with him to ensure he couldn't escape. The detective waved an officer over to them and whispered in Czech. The officer eyed Pierce and nodded.

"This is Officer Videvic. He will go with you."

The officer motioned for Pierce to lead the way, and Pierce walked across the square to Cafe Mozart with Videvic close behind. The two men ascended the stone staircase around a glass-walled elevator into the café on the second floor.

Café Mozart was decorated in Victorian-style wallpaper and dark wood furniture. The window beside Pierce overlooked the intricate Astronomical Clock of Prague.

A waiter approached them and glanced at the police officer beside Pierce.

"Table?"

"No," Pierce said. "We'll only be a minute. Where is the toilet?"

"Hallway past reception. Last door on the right, sir."

Pierce turned to the expressionless officer. "Just need to wash the blood off my hands."

The officer nodded. Pierce walked down the beige marble hallway to the door. He knew that if there was a window, he could get out, and if there wasn't, he could wait for the police officer, knock him out, and stuff him into a stall while he fled to his awaiting plane at the airport.

Inside the bathroom, Pierce found four brass-hinged windows above the sink. The one on the right didn't open.

Shit.

The left window lever turned with a squeak, and Pierce pulled it open. Just below the window, a series of thin, metal platforms connected to the next building only four feet away. He hopped onto the counter and slid through the small window onto the metal plates meant to bridge the small divide between the buildings. He let his weight down onto the metal, and it gave way. A loud clang scattered nearby pigeons into the air.

He pushed his other foot off the windowsill and leaped to a nearby concrete pillar with a series of steel steps protruding from it. He latched onto one of the steel bars and twisted his body toward the post, then climbed up to the roof above and raced to a pipe at the rear edge of the building. A thick, maroon drainage pipe sprouted from the roof at his feet. He turned and embraced the dusty drainage pipe and inched his way down the back wall of Café Mozart.

Two stories below, Pierce reached cobblestones beside an old pizza restaurant tucked into in a tiny alleyway. Crouching under the windows, he fled to the right. The alley emptied into another narrow street where construction equipment coughed diesel fumes into the cool morning air. To his left, the Old Town Square sat amongst a mass of police lights and commotion. He sprinted to the right, away from the square and into a now-bustling street.

Slipping into a souvenir store that had just been opened to his right, Pierce pulled out his wallet.

"Large hoodie?" Pierce asked.

"Yes, sir. We have."

"Great. I'll take one of these Prague University hoodies and one of these hats."

Pierce pulled a gray beanie off of a rotating rack. The beanie read 'CZECH' in large red letters and 'REPUBLIC' in smaller black letters.

He tossed 100 Euros on the counter and pulled the beanie onto his head. As he exited the store, he removed his suit jacket, threw it into a trash bin, and slid the hoodie over his white dress shirt.

A dozen uniformed police officers flooded the streets, scanning the crowd for Pierce. He knew they would be looking for people who didn't look like tourists; these men were experts at it. Their brains would work on autopilot to find anyone who stood out. Pierce began taking photos of the street with his phone and looking up at the spires and architecture. He knew if he sped up, they would notice the deviation from the crowd behavior. Andera wanted Pierce in custody. They would keep him in Prague, far from the work he needed to finish for HIG.

Thirty feet away, an officer neared the small group of people Pierce had joined. Pierce resorted to the two most effective methods that could be done to avoid detection in a pinch. He pulled eighteen inches of dental floss from a sewn pocket in his waistband, wrapped it several times around four fingers, and tucked the short coil of floss into his upper lip. Though it might be outdated, this technique could still defeat most facial recognition systems and change someone's face just enough to avoid detection.

As the second measure, Pierce opened his mouth to breathe. Dubbed the 'mouth breather' at HIG training, this technique sent a signal to the primitive part of the human brain that someone was not a threat. No one who's running from police—or is an immediate threat to others –

keeps their mouth open. It tricked the mind into thinking there was nothing to worry about.

The police officer approached the group, studying everyone he passed. Pierce stared at the officer with curious eyes, something bad guys and fugitives don't do. The officer made eye contact with Pierce, scanned the rest of the group, and kept walking.

Forty yards ahead, Pierce hailed a taxi on Karlova.

"Airport."

He updated HIG headquarters and retrieved his alternative United Nations credentials from his sling bag.

With a diplomatic flight clearance, neither the plane nor its passengers could be searched.

CHAPTER 5

YORKTOWN, VIRGINIA

Kelly pulled a skirt onto her narrow hips and slid her feet into a pair of tall heels before rushing out her front door and climbing into a Rideshare car waiting outside.

After a short ride from her apartment, she climbed out of the car into the warm breeze in front of the pub.

The five HIG students had agreed to meet Friday night at the Yorktown Pub, a small local favorite that sat beachside on the York River. Fridays were particularly crowded, but they managed to get a booth under an orange Coast Guard life ring on the wall.

Kelly surveyed the bar, profiling behaviors. A new habit. After a year of learning psychological tactics ranging from mind control and brainwashing to lie-detection and hypnosis, people looked different—more fragile. The *world* looked different.

She took comfort that the pub hadn't changed—the decorative concrete floors that looked like a school cafeteria met with wood-paneled walls covered in nautical decor, stickers, and a large wooden 'No Wake' sign. Ball caps from a hundred or so local Coast Guard guys sat on a shelf along the ceiling of the small bar that *maybe* held fifty people. After a year in Yorktown, Kelly had come to love the pub. Even in the loud bar, the peaceful feeling of Yorktown and the beach were only steps away. Over the course of a day, the clientele went from an upscale lunch crowd to a mix of young people and old-time regulars at night.

Her group settled into the booth and a prompt waitress appeared. Kelly ordered a glass of Pinot Grigio, and the other four ordered beers. Kelly, as was HIG tradition on the Friday evening before graduation, produced a permanent invisible ultraviolet marker from her small purse. The other students smiled. Kelly walked to the front corner of the bar to the right of the doors and signed her name invisibly in a spot near the 'No Wake' sign on the wall. She handed the marker off and watched her classmates do the same. She had never brought a blacklight to the bar, but she always imagined the dozens of signatures of HIG graduates on the walls of the Pub. Yorktown held more secrets than Washington, D.C.

After a few minutes, the others ran into locals they had come to know over the course of the year, and Kelly found herself alone, watching a tall man with shaggy hair pull a drunk girl out of the bar with more force than Kelly was comfortable with. They took a right and she watched them pass by the windows in the front of the pub. Kelly threw a crumpled Twenty on the table, pushed through the crowd, and followed them out. The man had shoved the girl onto the end of a long brown bench where she drunkenly sat. Her eyes weren't focused on anything as her head swung in little circles.

She's horribly drunk.

"Is this your girlfriend?" Kelly asked the tall man.

"She is tonight. Want to join us? I only live, like, three minutes from here," the man offered with a grin.

Kelly had already spotted a long-bladed pocketknife clipped to his jeans pocket.

"So, you guys just met?"

The man's face flashed anger. His jaw muscles tightened. He was right-handed. His dominant foot never moved backward, his nostrils never flared, and his fingers never so much as curled into his palms. He wasn't going to do anything.

"She's coming home with me. It's none of your goddamn business. We're fine. Why don't you get back inside? There's dangerous people out here."

You're right, she thought. *Just not who you think.*

For a moment, Kelly imagined using HIG Tradecraft on the man and making him drink water out of the ocean until he vomited, maybe making him swallow his own fist. He would have done anything she told him to. She only needed a few seconds with him.

"Listen, I get it. Let me at least get her to pay her tab so they don't call the *police*." The mention of police would make him more compliant, even if just for a moment.

Kelly didn't wait for permission. She took the woman by the arm and walked her inside. One of her HIG classmates spotted her walking in with the drunk girl and trotted over.

"What the hell, Kelly? You used Tradecraft on her in *public*?" he said.

"No. She's drunk. Sick perv outside was going to take her in his car to God knows where. Take care of her. I'll be right back."

"Need backup, Tinkerbell?"

Her small frame, sharp nose, and shoulder-length hair had earned her the nickname of 'Tinkerbell.' Kelly didn't turn back as she walked out, only threw up a dismissive no-big-deal wave.

The guy still stood outside the bar near a pile of empty beer kegs, waiting on his victim. Kelly approached him, her heels clicking on the small paved sidewalk. The man lit a cigarette as she neared.

"She's just paying now. Sorry to be all in your business earlier."

"No big deal, honey." He leaned sideways as he took a drag on the cigarette, eyeing her body. "I'd sure like to get my hands on that ass of yours, too."

Her stomach turned as she exhaled.

She stepped closer and leaned in. He pulled his cigarette from his mouth, his eyes widening with the excitement of a reptile about to devour prey.

"Listen. What's your name?" she said softly.

"Eddie."

"Listen, Eddie..." Kelly spoke to the man, a controlling hand on his shoulder. Eddie's head drooped down, and he nodded as Kelly sped through techniques she'd spent the last year honing. As she wrapped up, she noticed a blonde woman in a dark suit standing next to a black Suburban parked next to a lamp pole along the beach about thirty yards away.

Kelly brought Eddie back to consciousness. The woman in the suit stood waved Kelly over.

Shit. I'm toast.

She knew the vehicle. It was a HIG Suburban. The black hockey puck antenna on the hood gave it away.

She had just used her training in a way she had agreed on dozens of admissions papers not to, and the woman in the suit had seen it.

With her head down, she walked to the car and began apologizing. The woman in the suit held up a hand, interrupting her. Kelly hadn't met her before—students were kept separate from all of the HIG operators because of what she had learned this morning. This woman didn't work for the State Department. She was a ghost.

"The Director needs to see you," the woman cut in. "I'm Jennifer Goram, a senior operative at HIG."

The older woman's long blonde hair danced sideways in the wind as she extended a hand to Kelly, her suit jacket straining against her chest.

"Like the *Director*-Director?" Kelly's eyes widened. Her stomach churned.

"Yes. Message your friends you're okay and jump in. We're heading to HIG headquarters."

Kelly climbed into the passenger seat and immediately resumed apologizing. "I seriously didn't mean to do anything against regulations. I didn't even use anything dangerous on him."

"What *did* you do to that guy back there?" Jennifer raised an amused eyebrow.

"I-I just told him he'd be nicer to women for the rest of his life," she lied. And instantly regretted it. She'd just spent a year learning every lie-detection method known to man.

"Is that all? I couldn't really hear, but it looked like you were speaking for much longer than that." Jennifer eyed her with skepticism.

Kelly sighed in surrender. "I...gave him permanent erectile dysfunction."

Jennifer, still holding the wheel, let Kelly stew in suspense before she erupted in laughter so loud it made Kelly jump. "We all have to do it on occasion. You're in your last week of training, so you've been vetted. You're good. I probably would have done way worse."

"Jesus. This isn't why the Director wants to see me?" Kelly began to breathe again.

"Not at all. You're fine. I promise."

Following the weekend, the five students would graduate. That meant meeting other operatives, getting to meet the director, learning about the history of HIG, and, most importantly, what the *hell* HIG stood for.

The students had a running bet to determine the meaning of the acronym simply pronounced 'hig':

Human Influence Group

Humanitarian Intervention Group

Humanitarian Intelligence Governance

No one seemed to be able to agree on which was more likely, and the varying instructors who taught them assured them there was no possible way they would be able to know, guess, or even understand the name until graduation.

"We aren't allowed to meet the Director until after graduation. I'm not allowed to meet *you* until after graduation," Kelly stated. Hoping to glean more information from Jennifer.

"You know how powerful HIG is. With agents in most countries, the Director could have any missile launched from any country she wishes, at any target...and she can't pull your little ass out of training?"

"Good point," Kelly said, turning down the A/C. "I just wish I didn't smell like a bar."

CHAPTER 6
YORKTOWN, VIRGINIA

I haven't heard from you in 25 years. Today's your birthday, so – emailing as always. Happy birthday, Dad.

-P.

Pierce Reston shut the lid of his laptop. He had only been home from Prague an hour when he received a message asking him to report to HIG headquarters.

Sitting barefoot on a kitchen barstool in a disheveled suit, Pierce tilted a frozen bottle of vodka into the only cup he owned and surveyed his barren house as the cold liquid pulsed onto eager ice cubes.

It used to look like a family lived here. After the incident, he didn't see the point in keeping up the pretense. He'd gotten rid of almost everything he owned. Maps adorned the walls with thumbtacks and threads of different colors running to and from countries, explaining the inner workings of what had consumed his life. The long, gray living room walls around him were covered in more maps and six flat-screen televisions, each one tuned to a different news channel and muted.

His bedroom boasted a single mattress and a bedside table. He had all he needed to live.

Pierce gazed past his reflection in the window, out into the dark woods behind his house, but was jarred back to the present by a vibrating phone on the counter.

A message flashed on the screen from the former director of HIG, Alex Frost.

Can you be here in 45?

- *Will do.*

Alex had been Pierce's mentor, recruiter, and trainer at HIG. He'd discovered Pierce while Pierce had been working for the CIA as an intelligence analyst, back when he believed no agency was more secretive or powerful than the CIA.

"It's like the Federal Reserve," Alex had said, "except secret and with people who are smart."

After a hot shower, Pierce packed a new go-bag. He pushed his dark brown hair aside and loaded the last of several weapons into the rectangular backpack.

He pulled his coat over a slim, button-down white shirt, picked up his keys, and got into his twelve-year-old Jaguar, bound for HIG headquarters.

CHAPTER 7
YORKTOWN, VIRGINIA

Deidra Collins drowned in her thoughts. She walked through the gargantuan kitchen at HIG headquarters, her heels echoing off the stone interior walls of the quiet mansion as she entered the living room.

In the well-lit room, Deidra took a seat on the brown leather couch across from Alex Frost, the man whom she'd relieved as Director of HIG. Deidra crossed her legs and leaned back as the two of them sat in silence.

Alex had become an old man since Deidra began at HIG. At seventy, his skin had the wear of decades in the sun, and she had watched his hair turn from black to gray over the years.

He looked at her with fatherly eyes. "We'll get this figured out. Pierce should be here soon."

Deidra nodded. She had only just replaced Alex as the director of HIG and was the first black woman to hold the position. Even though she was an older woman with a lifetime of experience at HIG, she was terrified she would screw something up. She wanted her legacy at HIG to stay untarnished.

Deidra slid her leather portfolio onto the thick glass coffee table between them. "We've got a lot to deal with here, and Pierce needs help. With what happened in Prague, and now all of this, we need to nail this down quick."

Alex nodded. Deidra continued, "I can't pull agents off the Saudi deal now; we've got thirty-nine shipments of chemical and bioweapons from Syria that need to disappear. I'd like to send Kelly Kennedy with Pierce to figure out what's going on."

Alex rubbed his face as he took in a contemplative breath. "You'd like to send a *student*?"

"She's graduating Monday, Alex. She's the best option we have right now."

"What's the most recent update on the situation?"

Deidra pulled her leather portfolio off the table, flipped it open, and slid her reading glasses on.

"According to several therapy call centers and four police reports, nineteen people complained of 'disappearing time'; they had several days of gaps in their memory. This might be common, but the incidence of it all happening in two major cities was enough to make me worry that something was happening—someone was erasing those memories deliberately. With the incident at the hotel in Prague and this all happening here, we need answers. It might be nothing, but if it turns out to be someone using HIG methods, we have a compromise, and Pierce will need help."

Alex leaned forward on the leather couch. "Kelly's an impressive girl. In less than a year, her skills have outgrown several of the instructors who've been doing this a long time."

"I like her. You like her. She can operate," Deidra offered.

Alex lifted his eyebrows and nodded. "You're the Director. This is your show now. I gave up that spot so I could relax, but I agree with you. She's phenomenal."

Deidra exhaled in relief. "Good. I sent Jennifer to pick her up thirty minutes ago."

CHAPTER 8

YORKTOWN, VIRGINIA

The Suburban's headlights illuminated the densely wooded streets on the way to HIG. As they neared the mysterious building she was never able to visit as a trainee, Kelly's hands started to sweat, and her heart rate climbed.

Jennifer broke the silence. "Tonight, you're going to meet Pierce Reston. He's one of the senior operators. Absolutely *awesome* guy."

"Wow. What's going on?"

"They need you to begin operating just to go look into some stuff. Pierce or the Director will brief you at HIG. It's pretty cool actually. You'll get a chance to operate before any of your classmates do. With Pierce—" Jennifer seemed to hesitate. "Don't mention shootings. Like mass shootings."

"It's not really my go-to conversation topic, but I'll make sure not to touch it. I'm guessing he's sensitive about that?"

Jennifer turned onto a dirt road and shot an uneasy glance at Kelly. "He was engaged to a deaf woman, Anna. We *all* loved her. Long story short, she was in a shopping mall in Richmond when a shooting occurred. She was in the restroom at the time it all started. She didn't know the shooting was happening, and walked into the hallway the shooters were hiding in. It changed him."

Kelly sat for a moment in silence, watching the woods give way to a clearing ahead. "Jesus."

"Just wanted to mention it. It was two years ago, but you'll be working with Pierce, and it's something you should know."

"Thank you, Miss Goram."

"Call me Jennifer."

As they entered the clearing, a sprawling mansion appeared with balconies, terraces, granite walls and a long, imposing Victorian roofs atop the many connected structures. Lights illuminated the building from below, making it glow in contrast with the night sky.

Jennifer, seeing Kelly's mouth open, offered a brief introduction. "The property was given to HIG by Thomas Paine, the lost Founding Father of America. He brought HIG to the US, but it was founded in the 1500s. We've been based *here* since the 1700s; the first time HIG was used to do what the letters *actually* stand for."

Jennifer pulled into the long gravel driveway and parked under a covered archway at the side of the mansion.

Both women got out of the vehicle and Jennifer swiped a badge on a small metal plate beside the door. A loud click sounded, and Kelly followed Jennifer inside.

A long hallway with a white marble floor led to a giant kitchen with towering brick walls and vaulted ceilings. The house smelled like new paint and fresh coffee.

As the women walked down the echoing beige hall, Jennifer introduced Kelly to HIG.

"Privacy is obviously pretty important to HIG. We've had penetration attempts that date back to 1872. Some even earlier in the 1500s. The house is lined in six layers of copper mesh, and all the windows vibrate to prevent the use of laser listening devices. You can even feel it on the glass. It's creepy. All those chimneys you saw on the roof, they are mostly fake. It's artificial brick covering antennas and jammers."

Jennifer and Kelly walked across the large kitchen to the living room. Kelly eyed the arrangement of three leather couches positioned around a glass and wood coffee table that must have weighed more than her car. The two people sat across each other on leather couches stood as Kelly approached; Alex shot her a warm smile.

"This is Deidra Collins. Director of HIG."

Kelly extended a nervous hand and introduced herself to the most powerful woman on Earth. Deidra's neat ponytail fell onto a crisp white business jacket. Although she was an older woman, she still looked like an athlete and could probably outperform half the people half her age.

"Hi, Kelly. Welcome aboard. Very proud of you. We will fill you in in just a sec." Deidra's voice was authoritative and still warm.

A beep emitted from the kitchen.

"There's Pierce," Deidra announced.

Pierce came through the hallway into the kitchen and made his way to the living room. Kelly stared. His short hair was pushed over as if he'd been woken up recently. His sharp suit framed his lean shape. His steel-gray eyes met with Kelly's; she tucked her hair behind her right ear and adjusted her posture.

"Kelly, this is Pierce Reston. He's one of our senior operators here," Deidra announced as Pierce stepped into the room.

"I've heard good things, Miss Kennedy," Pierce said. "You have a reputation."

Kelly introduced herself, trying not to stare. She remembered what Jennifer had revealed about him in the car. Her smile softened, even as her stomach twisted.

They all sat. Deidra wasted zero time and began the briefing.

"We've got multiple indicators that someone may be using HIG methods who isn't one of us. It could be a coincidence, but I doubt it. The strongest indicators are people in Houston, Texas and San Jose, California reporting missing time. Dissociative Amnesia. Aside from this, we have five marketing researchers who are either dead or missing. Before they died or disappeared, they uploaded tons of research into some kind of overseas server."

Dissociative Amnesia. Kelly remembered it well from training. Someone would remember all of Monday, and they wake up and it's Friday–missing time. Operatives, including Kelly, were taught to create this in people if they feared HIG could be compromised. There were four other reasons they were authorized to use it, but they were rare. One of them was to prevent nuclear emissions of any kind. It was, by far, one of the more dangerous things she had been taught at HIG. What scared Kelly most was that they didn't always work equally on everyone. It was up to the operator to adjust their technique and to perform a series of tactics designed to enhance human suggestibility.

"Listen, Kelly. I don't have time to keep you humble here. You're the brightest we've had in a long time, and I need you and Pierce to head to Houston. The missing marketing people are in the same cities where people have been reporting stolen or missing time. We've got the reports and I'll send them to your phones.

"Everyone missing is either a marketing expert or a marketing psychology researcher. The one I *can't* explain is this thing in Prague. Pierce will fill you in on the ride. The helicopter will be here in..." Deidra glanced at her watch, "fifteen minutes. Kelly, I've had your go-bag collected from your apartment, along with your identity kit. Please keep in mind this could very well be nothing, but it has the potential to be a real compromise."

CHAPTER 9

YORKTOWN, VIRGINIA

Pierce was exhausted. With any luck, he would be able to sleep on the plane. After a brief discussion regarding the mission, Jennifer and Kelly walked outside to retrieve her bags and prep their equipment for the short flight to the Newport News airport, where a HIG jet awaited them on the runway.

Deidra walked to the kitchen, and Pierce turned to Alex, who somehow predicted what he was thinking and said, “She’s not a babysitter, Pierce. She’s our top pick from this year’s class. We’ve got everyone wrapped tight around Syria right now and I can’t pull those agents for an assignment that may not pan out.”

"I'm not an investigator, Alex. I'm an operative. These turn out to be a coincidence every time you send someone out. I have no interest in going to Houston."

Alex held up a hand. "You tell me you're not an investigator. You really think I don't know what you do in your free time?"

"What the hell does that mean?"

Alex paused before responding in his fatherly tone. "I've been in your house, Pierce. The maps on your walls, the televisions. There's a pin in every city there's been a major shooting. Three pieces of furniture, no carpets or curtains. Frankly, between you and me, you need to hire a goddamn decorator."

Pierce allowed himself to look embarrassed before speaking. "I've told you before, those shootings are connected. I just need more time. There's a massive pattern we know from history for this—from the guy who killed John Lennon, the guy who murdered Bobby Kennedy, to almost every single shooting. They almost all report hearing voices. Most of them report the same voice, being told to kill a specific person. Even the congresswoman who was shot. The lawsuit following the shooting stated, and I quote, 'illegally hand-picked to be a sleeper assassin.'"

"You've been putting all this together?" Alex stared at Pierce in wonder. "Why didn't you bring this up to me?"

"I needed time. The case is compelling already, but I don't want you thinking I'm crazy. Everything I've got is rock solid."

"We'll look into it when you guys come back from Houston. Jesus, just bring this stuff to me. You've got enough to deal with as it is. Shoveling this stuff alone isn't helpful. Let's use our resources here. You're going to Houston, Pierce. And that girl you think is your babysitter, *I* found her. *I* recruited her. She's got more talent than you *ever* did." Alex smiled.

The door beeped; Pierce peered into the kitchen. Above the stove, an eighteen-foot-long oil painting of men on horses dominated the tall stone wall. "The Surrender of Lord Cornwallis." A sobering reminder of what operatives committed to when they joined HIG. The painting depicted two rows of a dozen or so men on horseback facing each other. In the middle, a single man on a horse towered over three men. The man on the horse was the American General Lincoln. The men standing beside the horse were British Generals, preparing to officially surrender to the United States of America. Cornwallis, the British Lord who surrendered his troops, never showed up for the surrender; he was sitting with a HIG operative in a cave just a hundred yards from where the Yorktown Pub stood today.

The painting always made Pierce leave HIG with a renewed dedication to his work.

"There are the girls," Alex said. He faced Pierce before Deidra and Kelly made it to the kitchen.

"I need you to get to the bottom of this. Go to Houston. Figure this out. Chopper will be here in three minutes."

*****

"The Mary Celeste," Alex said, looking at Kelly.

Kelly looked around, hoping someone would fill her in.

"Kelly, you've been glancing at the *same* painting since you came in."

She looked back at the simple painting of the ship on the wall. "Yes, sir. It's—just so different from all of the more Victorian-looking paintings in here. I like it."

"Technically, the painting is of a ship called 'Amazon' in 1861. Her name was changed to Mary Celeste later. One of our first HIG training manuals on overthrowing tyrannical governments was aboard that vessel, a book published that year under the name *Mental Medicine*. A HIG manual was hidden within its pages. The ship set sail from New York, bound for Italy in 1872, where our Italian HIG members would attempt to overthrow what was slowly becoming a dictatorship.

"The book was also gone. For almost a century, HIG had assumed a compromise had occurred. Now we think another ship tried to stop them from bringing it to Italy, and the captain took the book to the ocean floor with him to protect it. The abandoned ship was found adrift four hundred miles from where they should have been, and nothing on the ship was disturbed."

CHAPTER 10
SAN JOSE, CALIFORNIA

After four tours in the Middle East, Trent Cavanaugh finally got shot. In the head.

Trent had seen the worst of humanity. From people cannibalizing fellow villagers in the deserts of the Middle East to mothers who begged soldiers to take their child, knowing no matter what happened, their baby would have a better life somewhere else.

When Trent got shot, he didn't feel it. The bullet hit him in the side of the head. Luckily, his communications headset took most of the damage. His skull was fractured, but he considered himself the luckiest son of a bitch on

Earth. It was after the brain scans that the doctors told him he had a Mild Traumatic Brain Injury.

He was pulled immediately from combat duty and surreptitiously medically retired from the Marine Corps. They told him his behavior had become erratic and that he needed to take medications to counteract the effects of the brain injury, but they were idiots. Trent had seen doctors before. He had no faith in them. Even national statistics said they were wrong about most of the shit they told patients. They just Google every fucking thing they hear from a patient. If you do that, *every* website tells you you're going to die.

He refused to believe any of them. He didn't have a brain injury, he just got angrier more easily because he was tired of the bullshit. But every doctor he'd seen told him he had a brain injury, like a choir of morons.

Following his discharge, he sunk into a depression. It made him excommunicate his entire family for being 'negative' about his condition and he eventually found a job with *Grossman Ural*, a United States defense contractor.

After guarding a site in Israel on the Palestinian border for a year, he was fired for inappropriate outbursts, and was eventually approached with a job offer by a man who Trent still believed was the scariest man he had ever met: Aphid. The man had no other name and insisted that Trent address him by it and nothing else. After living with the most dangerous men on Earth and fighting some of the most elite warriors in the Middle East, the seventy-year-old man still terrified him. Despite the man's thin frame, gray hair, and calm demeanor, Trent could smell a monster.

Trent continued to grow out his beard, and, despite his Irish heritage, he had a darker skin tone, which he was grateful for, especially when in the Middle East. He finally found an employer who valued the work he did and didn't give a shit about office politics.

Aphid introduced Trent to the *real* way the world worked. He had an entire team of hard men like Trent who were all paid more than any defense company could hope to pay them.

Aphid's men would die for him. He hired out of the Private Military Contractors (PMC) circles, and never took in anyone without ensuring they were an 'apex predator'–men at the top of the food chain.

He paid well and commanded respect without ever so much as raising his voice.

It was only forty-eight days into working for Aphid that Trent was asked to perform a 'clean-up' job; a politician in Brussels had agreed to vote a certain way in a political move and went back on his promise.

The guy in Brussels had a family, but that's how shit works when you're dishonorable. Trent had simply broken into his hotel room in Dubai and proceeded to shoot him one bullet at a time until the man perished.

Death before dishonor.

Life was a chess game, and Trent had become a bishop. He was given a lot of latitude by Aphid to operate his own way, and he never violated the man's trust–until a few weeks ago, when Trent was asked to retrieve a video file..

The video was kept in a server room in Budapest. It was secured thirty feet underneath two large, white water tanks one and a half kilometers southwest of the Budapest Airport terminal building. The company running the secure server operated under the water plant and enjoyed a temperature twelve degrees cooler than most server rooms due to the depth underground and the water overhead.

Aphid tasked him *in person* with the job. He gave Trent a kit containing all of the underground building diagrams and security procedures, along with everything else he needed to extract the video from the server. After this, however, Aphid leaned in and spoke to Trent with a look of cold, black granite.

"If you see, listen to, or open this video file, I'll cut up everyone you've ever met in front of you, and feed them to you."

He had never threatened Trent before. Aphid wanted this video to himself. And it made Trent curious.

The file sat dormant in the underground facility for months. Aphid had left it there to observe if anyone would come for it. Nothing. Only a week ago, Trent had taken the file.

He had planned ahead. His military training had taught him how to plan missions exactly like this. He never imagined he'd use it as an assassin.

Two guards rotated shifts inside and outside the facility. They carried AK47s each with only one magazine. One guard would go into the facility while the other took watch at the door at the west end of the water tower's footprint. Inside, a set of concrete stairs led to another secure door that opened to the underground ghost server room. The guards looked overweight, and low on discipline. They'd sit in plastic chairs outside the door with their rifles in their laps, smoking cigarettes most of the time. The moon wasn't due to rise for another hour, and the darkness would help him get in and out faster.

Trent entered the woods lining the road just southeast of the target area and made his way through a hole in the eastern fence at a weak point where a water pipe exited the facility.

Skirting the fence in the dark, Trent found another tree line just ten yards north of the water tanks and made a quick sprint to the northwest corner of the area. The tiny, white guard shack stood only sixty yards in front of him.

The guard sat in his chair on the opposite side of the small shack that housed the stairs leading down to the server. Dodging the floodlights, Trent sprinted to the back end of the shack. He stopped and listened intently while he caught his breath. Cigarette smoke permeated the air. A thin, black wire on the corner of the shack ran up to a security camera that captured the entrance to the hidden server rooms below. Trent carefully pulled a wire cutter from his vest and clipped the wire with a barely audible *click*.

He moved to the side of the shack and could see the boots of the guard he had been stalking for two days protruding from behind the wall. Trent moved forward, advancing on his target in a slow, predatory crouch. The guard scrolled through pornographic images on his phone as he flicked his cigarette into a coffee can beside him.

Trent slowly withdrew the silenced .22 pistol from his holster, keeping his eyes locked on the man, and dropped him with a single shot to the base of his skull.

The security guard's body slouched. Trent caught his rifle before it fell off his lap. He was so close to the airport that a single gunshot ringing out through the open landscape would trigger alarms he didn't need.

Trent pulled him upright in the plastic chair and removed the keycard to the building from the man's pocket.

The door opened without a sound. Trent descended the concrete steps in silence to the second door below. He paused for a moment, listening for footsteps inside. Nothing.

He slid the keycard into the black, plastic slot and the door clicked open. He pushed the door aside with one hand and readied his pistol with the other. White light flooded the isolated stairwell from inside the facility. Trent pushed past the door into a bright hallway that extended out to his left and right. His recon had revealed that three men worked in the server rooms aside from the two guards; they wore lab coats when they exited the building after their shifts. Trent took the hallway to the right and approached the first room. He inched himself along the wall. Papers rustled in the room ahead of him just before he heard a heavy cough. He rounded the open doorway and found a worker in a white lab coat in a small office. The worker sat at a metal desk against the wall shuffling through a manila envelope. He began coughing again, and Trent used his second cough to mask the sound of one more bullet.

Two down. Three to go.

At the back wall of the office, the door to the primary server room hung open. He navigated through the office and found himself at the doorway. Cold air fell from the room, and the sound of hundreds of tiny computer fans consumed the space. Electronics buzzed through a thick smell of cigarettes, and curry.

Trent entered the room at the ready. Another worker in a lab coat crouched at a terminal; his eyes widened as he tried to stand. His mouth opened, and Trent squeezed the trigger. The quiet pistol spat a bullet through the man's head and into the machinery beyond him. A startled sound rattled from the rear of the room behind the other server racks.

Trent scanned the area and stepped back to walk down the next row of humming electronics. The second guard sat on a couch that had been covered in a white sheet at the far end of the server room. He tossed a clipboard onto the floor in front of him, leaning his body sideways, trying to identify the sound, maybe waiting for a second one. He raised his head and his eyes met Trent's. As the guard reached for the rifle beside him, Trent exploded into a sprint forward and emptied the remaining ten rounds in his magazine.

Without a second glance at the body, Trent reloaded his weapon and continued his search.

Four down, one to go.

With the first server room cleared, Trent returned to the hall and entered the second server room to find no one. He backed out and silently crept through the hall toward the only remaining room—the restroom.

As he neared the door, a toilet flushing echoed in the hall. He slid along the wall and stood next to the doorway of the restroom. The remaining worker inside finished up, and as he opened the door to exit, Trent fired a single bullet into his head.

He walked back into the first server room and unfolded a laminated map of the facility. His target file was in the first bank of servers, in the third rack from the bottom.

He inserted a thumb drive into the protruding receptacle and the light on the thumb drive turned red. After about thirty seconds, it flashed to orange, indicating it had a grip on whatever file it was designed to locate. Trent kept his pistol leveled at the door. After a long minute passed, the light finally went green.

He exited the facility the same way he entered, staring at the data drive in his hand, mesmerized by the small, weightless file he was forbidden to view. He put the drive into a jacket pocket and made the quick trip back to the Stacio Airport Hotel.

Trent was about to violate the trust of the one man he had finally managed to respect.

He prepared his hotel room by activating the power on his handheld eight-antenna jammer. It jammed signals for every phone, Wi-Fi, and Bluetooth device within about twenty-two meters. If any of his actions got back to Aphid, he'd be dead in a day.

Trent jabbed the small drive into his computer's USB port, and, to his delight, a folder containing the file appeared. The file size was much larger than it should have been for a fourteen-minute video. After a moment of hesitation, Trent clicked the file and a movie began playing on his laptop. The movie was an old-looking black and white film of a family at a dinner table. It was apparently made to teach table manners to children. Hidden in the background, in the corner of the room, was a shelf with family photos on it. One of the pictures, Trent noticed, looked like another embedded video of moving images within the picture frame.

Some kind of embedded video.

The next morning, he took it immediately to a tiny, local computer repair shop about a mile east of the airport. The lone shop owner assured Trent he could pull the embedded video from the file. Trent ensured the man's computers had no connection to the internet.

Over the course of an hour, the man produced a grainy video of the little rectangle containing the hidden audio and video while Trent stood beside him and smoked cigarettes. He had to pay the guy seven hundred dollars cash for his silence, and then a single bullet, making it free. Trent also took the computers used to do the job and casually dumped them in a local river on the way back to Hotel Stacio.

The man's death served a greater good; Trent needed to know what he was delivering to Aphid.

Trent made it back to the hotel in time to pack his bags, turn the jammer on, and place his iPad onto the desk to watch the forbidden video. What he saw shook him and he didn't know why. It was a confusing video of an older man teaching the viewer how to say a sentence he called 'Phrase Seven,' a twelve-word phrase, spoken while touching someone simultaneously on the shoulder. The bizarre man also seemed to place a great deal of importance on accurately speaking these words. The phrase was obviously important for some reason, so Trent memorized it.

He closed the lid on his iPad and sent the video to Aphid.

Before getting on a plane to Houston the following day, Trent Cavanaugh unfolded a small, waterproof notebook from his pocket, twisted his pen, and wrote down the strange sentence he'd heard in the video, not realizing it could kill more people than any plague in history

CHAPTER 11

HOUSTON, TEXAS

The Gulfstream GV jet's landing shook Pierce awake. Sunrise lit the cabin in a soft, orange glow. Kelly had obviously been awake for a while—unable to sleep. She poured a cup of coffee for Pierce and handed it across the small aisle to him.

Pierce balanced the cup as he repositioned his seat upright. Kelly gave him a barely concealed, *I'm-on-my-first-mission-and-I-can't-contain-myself* kind of smile. "We've got about eight minutes until we hit the hangar. Want to get cleaned up?"

Pierce eyed her suspiciously. "I don't look cleaned up?"

"You look like you've been sleeping on a plane for hours. Your toiletry bag's in the bathroom. I hung it on the mirror."

Pierce took an abundant swallow of the coffee and pulled out his phone, tapping out a message to HIG.

Arrived. Commencing assignment.

The jet turned into a large hangar where a white Police SUV sat, the engine running.

Pierce exited the bathroom in a crisp, charcoal gray suit, coffee in hand.

Kelly looked him up and down and promptly glanced away. Her cheeks reddened, but Pierce ignored it.

"Let's get going. We are heading to a crime scene in West Houston. It's about an hour's drive from here."

"We have a driver?" Kelly said, inspecting the hangar through her window.

Pierce peered out the window. "No, we don't. But Aaron and Valerie do. You're Valerie by the way."

"I figured. Who are Aaron and Valerie, exactly?"

Pierce unzipped his laptop bag and produced two sealed plastic bags. Each contained a set of credentials identifying them as Aaron Brown and Valerie Thomas, with the Texas Department of Public Safety–Forensics Unit (Crime Lab Services).

"We shouldn't need to use any Tradecraft here. How's your southern accent?"

Kelly opened the package with wide eyes, sifting through the dozens of documents and ID cards.

"I actually grew up in Arkansas. I worked for years to get rid of this little accent," she said in a drawn-out, southern tone.

"I think it sounds trustworthy," Pierce replied. "Let's leave all personal electronics here on the plane."

"Got it."

Kelly gently handed her cell phone to Pierce. The headphone jack on her phone had scratches around it from years of repetitive use.

Introverted. Likes music. Needs personal space. Might have had parents with limited money–a two-year-old phone without a single scratch, save for the headphone jack. She takes good care of her things.

Kelly wore a gray skirt, white blouse, and heels. Perfect for the job. Their training taught them to present themselves as banal as possible, and Kelly had already acclimated. Pierce understood now why Alex always had a faint smile when he talked about her.

"The guy out there is Houston Police Department. The pilots change the tail number and overall look of the plane at around 10,000 feet before we land based on the mission."

"Woah. Cool. How?"

"The plane has a bunch of exterior panels that use the same technology as an eBook reader. Black and white that looks just like text. The pilots can program any tail number we need based on the mission."

Pierce watched Kelly conceal an excited grin. She enjoyed the spy stuff.

Pierce dragged a large tackle box from the overhead storage compartment and placed it on the seat. It bore the official logo of the Texas

Department of Public Safety. "This is our forensics kit for the day."

The pilot opened the door and lowered the small staircase onto the polished floor of the empty hangar. The police officer strode over to the plane.

"I thought you guys had a bigger team," the heavy-set, tan officer said, greeting Pierce and Kelly at the base of the steep stairs.

Pierce glanced back into the plane before saying, "Just us today, as far as I know. How you been, Bill? It's Aaron Brown. You haven't met Valerie yet. Let me introduce you to Special Agent Valerie Thomas." He placed a hand on Kelly's back.

Kelly shook the officer's hand. "Please, just call me Val."

Officer Bill tipped his cowboy hat as he greeted her.

Pierce had memorized enough of Bill's details on the flight to convince the man that they had met, at least in passing.

"Bill. Been a few years since I've seen you. How's. . .Tiffany, right?"

The officer's eyebrows raised. "She's really good. Been a while for sure. Glad y'all are here."

They walked to the vehicle and Pierce put a hand on Bill's shoulder. "Bill, listen, you guys work your asses off down here, and there's not a single desire for me or Valerie to interfere. We're both more than happy to sit in the background. The boss only wants us to feed information back to Austin. Apparently, this missing woman made a lot of campaign contributions to the right people."

Bill nodded.

"Okay, Aaron, Val, hop on in. We'll head down there, and I'll brief you on the ride."

Bill turned the lights and sirens on to get them down to the crime scene.

A woman had gone missing, but had uploaded years of her marketing research to an unknown server before her disappearance. She was the senior marketing officer for a national advertising company, RainMaker. Her upload was a collection of all the company's confidential research on marketing and marketing psychology. As far as anyone had been able to tell, she had uploaded the data to a secure file transfer service no one was able to locate.

As they pulled up to the large, stone house, Pierce noted five other patrol cars and one solid black Chevy Suburban sitting out front. It had normal plates, but the small antennas on the back of the vehicle told Pierce it was local, not federal. The feds rarely had those; they relied *heavily* on cellular networks.

The officer put the SUV in park in front of the driveway. "Guys ready?"

Pierce and Kelly grabbed their equipment and walked up the drive. It was a massive stone house with gas-lit lanterns perched above a grand, towering wooden door.

The house was immaculate. Hardwood floors and ornate rugs were illuminated by sunlight streaking through large glass windows. Every couch and table had been arranged with decorations and books in flawless, organized rows. It looked like a compilation of every good housekeeping magazine.

Officer Bill walked them over to a taller man in a sharp police uniform.

"Chief, you remember Aaron Brown, I'm sure, and this is Miss Valerie Thomas with DPS Forensics."

The taller man extended a hand to them both. "Art Powell, Chief of Police."

Pierce and Kelly both shook his hand. Pierce had looked through the Chief's online posts on the ride over and complimented him on a few anti-gang initiatives he'd discussed on social media.

"Chief, we won't be long, just wanted to look around if *that's okay with you.* I've also got this young'un here I need to train up."

Pierce nodded his head while saying the words 'that's okay with you,' and touched his chest to make the Chief feel as though he was being sincere. Kelly smiled as Pierce called her young'un.

The Chief showed them the home office. It was ornately furnished and smelled like leather and wood. The scent brought him back to his days in the fancy HIG classroom. The Chief shrugged as they entered the office.

"Unless you're the digital forensics team, I don't know how much there is to see. The only thing we're really worried about is where the upload went. It looks like a server over in Europe, but no one has been able to tell me for sure yet. Miss Ferris is a bigtime friend of the Governor and occasionally helps out the Mayor quite a bit. We've got everyone we can working the case. I imagine that's why you guys are here."

"Chief, any threats or indications of a desire to leave town? Do you know if there's a security system in the house? Cameras and such?"

The Chief leaned against the large desk and shook his head. "Well, I can certainly tell you she left her house in her car. The prints we found on the alarm panel and the video from the doorbell camera confirm we have a –" he pulled out a small pocket-sized notebook. "--Catherine Norris, who's our lead suspect right now. But I can't figure out *why*. Catherine Norris is a young schoolteacher. Teaches at the elementary school here on Brittmoore. Catherine was captured on the doorbell camera. She rings the doorbell and tells miss Ferris she's running from an abusive boyfriend. Miss Ferris lets her into the house, and forty-two minutes later, both women leave in Miss Ferris' Lexus SUV. I'm not sure what to make of any of this. Catherine Norris teaches first grade, and she's every parent's favorite."

Pierce shook his head in confusion. "Chief, is there anything that indicated violence or that Miss Ferris was forced to send those uploads?"

The Chief stared at the green carpet and shook his head. "We haven't seen anything that seems to show any force was used. Far as I can tell, these two women don't know each other at all. For right now, we are considering Miss Norris, the schoolteacher, to be a suspect in the theft of the intellectual property, and we are telling officers to approach with caution if they find the vehicle." He scratched his face. "There's one more thing I don't understand. Miss Norris has no boyfriend we could find, and she came straight here after going to a *comedy club*. She went out with a few girlfriends last night to the comedy club and came *straight* here to this house."

A woman leaned into the office and held a phone toward the Chief.

"Excuse me, guys," he said as he walked away.

Pierce and Kelly stood alone in the room. The spacious home office reminded Pierce of the board game 'Clue.' The green carpets and dark wood walls wrapped around the room, and an unnecessarily large wooden desk sat in the center with a single green desk lamp next to the laptop.

"Their computer forensics has already been here and copied the hard drive. Might be why the mouse is on the left of the laptop."

Kelly gave Pierce a puzzled look. "Left side?"

"Yeah. Two photos of her in the hall. The victim was right-handed. One of them was a photo from behind her; she was twisted around to look at the camera, and her cell phone was in her right rear pocket. In another, she had a pen in her right hand while she spoke at some kind of convention."

Kelly raised her eyebrows.

"Wow. Okay, if we go through this computer, we can pull what was sent. All we need is the exact server address it was sent to."

"We need the *why*, Miss Valerie. Why did this happen? Why did it happen the night before she disappeared? It was her entire life's work. Three gigabytes of confidential research into marketing psychology and social media advertising research. And someone is suddenly so interested in marketing psychology research that they're doing stuff like this to get it. This woman decides after seeing a comedy show that she's *randomly* going to show up at this house, steal all of her research, and then kidnap her."

Kelly nodded, tossing her dark hair from her face as she turned to the door. She picked up her forensics tackle box, "I'll get the files from the guys outside."

The police had set up a small tent command center in the driveway beside the house, where they had arranged a row of computers. The department had assigned all available officers to the case. A case like this would be at the top of everyone's online news feed in Texas for weeks.

Before Kelly exited the room, Pierce reminded her, "Try to go easy on the Tradecraft, Miss Valerie."

She nodded and walked out.

Pierce looked at the chair next to the desk, then pulled a small blacklight from his pocket. Most blacklights didn't illuminate much, as they were cheap and set at the higher end of the light spectrum, somewhere around 395 nm. His was set precisely at 365nm. The lower wavelength blacklights would illuminate around a hundred times more hidden material than a cheap one. Pierce learned this while working for the CIA, and he'd carried the light with him ever since. It had proven valuable and had once come in handy during a fight.

Shining it at the computer, Pierce found the small outline of something illuminated under the blacklight just to the right of the mouse. Three outlines of almost-perfect circles—less than an inch in diameter—marred the flawless wood of the desk in front of the laptop. On the floor, in front of the chair, another glowing outline. It glowed brighter than the rest. Pierce angled the light to the seat of the chair, and there, on the front edge, was a triangular, brightly glowing shape of *something* that had been invisible to everyone else.

This was a kidnapping.

Pierce walked outside to talk to Kelly and found her thanking two police officers.

"John, thank you so much." She touched his arm. "I'm grateful you can *feel okay to give everything to me.* This seems to be just a fascinating case to me. You guys must really just fall in love with your work with all this technology."

Kelly emphasized the words in her speech she intended for the man's subconscious to hear as a separate instruction. The unconscious brain would pick up on those shifts in tone and recognize it as its own command. The mind could not criticize or filter it to determine whether it was a wise choice or not.

Pierce watched Kelly subtly gesture to herself as she said the words 'fascinating' and 'fall in love,' making the officer unconsciously associate those ideas with her.

"Yes, ma'am. It's my pleasure," the officer replied, his eyes wide, barely blinking. He handed her a thumb drive.

"Thanks, officers. I'll be in touch this evening if I find anything, and I'll make sure it all goes directly through you to the State."

Kelly came down the driveway to where Pierce stood waiting. Just out of earshot of the police, he shot a glance at Kelly with a grin. "I think he was ready to marry you."

Kelly closed her eyes. "Okay, I *might* have overdone it."

Pierce retrieved his phone from his pocket and inserted a short cable that protruded from the charging port. Kelly handed the thumb drive to him and he plugged it into the cord.

"These will upload to HIG in about 20 minutes or so."

"Bill," Pierce called as they came down the driveway. "Can you drop us off at the Westin hotel on I-10?"

"You bet. Y'all jump in."

Kelly climbed into the back seat and Pierce sat next to the officer. As the SUV piloted through the wealthy neighborhood, Bill spoke up. "Y'all, I ain't seen something like this before. A bunch of marketing research seems pretty small to kidnap someone over."

"I agree, Bill." Pierce eyed the upload progress on his phone. "Marketing research used to be called propaganda."

"You mean like the communist posters and stuff?"

"Yes. A lot like that. It was in high demand in the 1920s. A man named Edward brought it out of the shadows. He engineered psychological techniques to make more women smoke, called 'The Torches of Freedom Campaign' and worked with companies all over the country to develop psychological tactics intended to change public opinion. He's written books on how to manipulate large groups of people."

"I had no idea."

"Most people didn't. This guy is the same man who invented the name 'Department of Defense,' to make it more palatable for the people instead of the 'War Department.' He specialized in the extreme persuasion of countries. Even wrote books on how to do it."

"These people collect so much data on us now, I bet it's ten times easier to manipulate people."

"I would imagine it to be the case," Pierce continued. "The strangest thing of all...the man was actually Sigmund Freud's nephew."

"Jesus," Kelly whispered from the back seat.

The officer pulled up to a large, covered valet area. Pierce and Kelly thanked him as they exited the vehicle into the humid Texas air.

Kelly's eyes beamed expectantly. "What's next?"

"We go to that comedy club," Pierce said.

"To track her down?"

"No," Pierce replied, slipping his phone back in his pocket. "She's dead. It was a professional."

CHAPTER 12
SAN JOSE, CALIFORNIA

Trent clicked on a high-resolution photo of a group of circus performers. Glasses and silverware clanked through the chatter of nearby tables in the restaurant.

Aphid used steganography—encoding massive amounts of data within the computer code of a high-resolution image—to transmit data.

The decryption process began, and Trent watched the small loading circle rotate slowly until the target package came into view on his screen.

Trent had never imagined someone could hide images, data, and even entire books-worth of information within a single photograph. The lines of computer code that created the image could be tweaked in order to hide all kinds of information that only a decryption key could reveal. It seemed more secure than even the encryption the *military* had used.

All of his target packages came in like this. The job in Houston was a detailed black-and-white image of Venice Beach. The job in Brussels came to his phone as a color-filled image of a hot air balloon festival.

Trent verified the information he needed and switched off the phone. His glass of Cabernet Sauvignon arrived, and the waiter set a dessert menu on the table. He watched an athletic-looking woman close her eyes. Her arm slowly lifted into the air, and he knew she was perfect. Trent eyed the woman closely. She was the one. He imagined what she would look like in a helpless pile on the floor and couldn't help but smile.

CHAPTER 13

PRAGUE, CZECH REPUBLIC

American girls always smelled different when they were unconscious.

Pavel Brozik was saved by Aphid. Three years prior, he was caught running a heroin shipment across the border in a delivery truck and faced some serious charges. With the threat of life in prison, he accepted Aphid's offer of help. Aphid saved his life, and for that, in his mind, he was forever in his debt.

Every few weeks, he'd get a call from Aphid's men, asking for new specimens to be delivered to the testing facility in Eastern Prague. He would pick them up at the airport and simply deliver them to a warehouse about three kilometers northeast. Of course, the specimens didn't always go easily. Aphid gave him some equipment, and he'd adapted methods over the course of the year to make things go smoother.

Aphid had specific criteria for what he considered a 'specimen'—English-speaking, preferably American or Canadian, and female. Only women. Sometimes it was girls about eighteen or nineteen years old, but mostly women in their early twenties.

He didn't know what happened to them when he dropped them off at the research facility. If Aphid was kind enough to save his life, Pavel had no right to ask questions.

He'd been delivering girls to Aphid for almost two months, and he quite enjoyed the feeling of it. It felt like a mission from a spy movie and it very much pleased him when he completed a mission. Once, Aphid himself had praised him for doing a great job. That day, Pavel marked it on the wall calendar in his kitchen and was reminded of it every time he left his apartment.

Earlier this morning, Pavel received an image of a vivid orange Monarch butterfly on his phone. He opened the app to decrypt it. His pulse quickened and his mind raced with excitement when he saw the request for a new specimen.

Pavel's routine was simple. He placed fake Rideshare app signs he ordered online in his windows and drove the circular laps of the Prague airport passenger pickup loop until an arriving female passenger waved him down, mistaking him for their ride. Men would wave at him, but Pavel ignored them.

Today, it only took three laps around the airport loop to find a specimen. A lucky day for him.

She was blonde, alone, and looked very American, holding two expensive suitcases, and wearing oversized sunglasses. She waved her hand and Pavel beamed. He pulled up as close to the woman as he could manage with the other Rideshare drivers blocking the curb.

He rolled his window down and acted as though he couldn’t read his phone screen, fumbling with his reading glasses. Pretending to fiddle with his phone while the woman waited for him to confirm her name, he feigned frustration, and the woman simply blurted out her name.

"Picking up Jessica?"

"Yes! Jessica! So sorry," Pavel confirmed with relief.

At this point, if they didn't respond in English, he would politely say no and drive off and make another loop.

"Oh god, thank you!" she exclaimed—in perfect English.

Pavel hopped out of the car and loaded her luggage into the trunk, keeping his hat downcast to minimize exposure to the cameras (a trick he'd learned from Aphid). The girl tugged to open the rear door in vain. He kept the doors locked on purpose; he didn't want her getting in until he was prepared to start the mission.

Pavel climbed into the driver's seat, unlocked the doors, and performed a fake, submissive apology.

Pavel had tightened the bolts on the car's rear doors to ensure they took some force to close. As planned, she got into the back seat, and when she tugged on the inside handle to shut the door, she pulled hard. The door shut, and her hand immediately jerked back toward her chest.

"Fuck!"

Pavel had nineteen needles embedded into the handle of the door, laced with oil, a Sodium Amytal and Propofol mixture. He apologized, acting as if she'd been pinched by a loose handle, and quickly began driving. They were usually unconscious, or completely helpless, within a minute, but Pavel still kept a stun gun beside him in case they didn't go out fast enough.

Before they left the airport, Pavel stopped at a traffic light, where he completed his next mandatory step. He twisted in his seat and found the girl unconscious in the back. She was thin, unlike most of the Americans. Freckles dotted across her nose and cheeks and colorful artificial flowers wove through her light blonde braids. He collected all of her electronics and stuffed them into a signal-blocking Faraday bag. No one on Earth could track her location or even place a call with her items in the bag.

He made the fifteen-minute drive to the warehouse, texting the number he'd been given as he made the last turn. The girl snored softly in the rear seat. She smelled like flowers and sweat.

As he approached the building's abandoned loading area, he rolled his window down and turned on his hazard warning lights, signaling to the men inside that he hadn't been followed. When he came to a stop, two men in ski masks exited the building, pointing small submachine guns at him. Pavel took the keys out of the ignition and hung them out of the window with his other hand on the wheel, just like he always did.

One man opened the back door and gently pulled the girl from the car, folding her limp, unconscious body over his shoulder. He carried her back into the warehouse through the steel door while the other man retrieved her luggage and belongings from the trunk.

When the steel door closed again, Pavel started the car and drove back to his dry-cleaning shop to finish up the night's financial records.

Another mission completed.

He smiled for the rest of the evening.

PHRASE SEVEN

CHAPTER 14
HOUSTON, TEXAS

Pierce and Kelly stood next to a tiled pillar under the covered valet area of the Westin hotel. Pierce glanced at his watch. They needed to update HIG.

His fiancée had given the watch to him just three days before the shooting. He loved it, but the second hand ticked so loudly that he couldn't wear it to bed. She never knew that, though. He'd discovered a lot about life being in love with a deaf woman. There were small things no one thought about. You couldn't yell from the bathroom when you were out of toilet paper or if there was no towel when you stepped out of the shower. People would continually ask Pierce to do things for her when they found out she was deaf, as if she was incapable of handling her own life. It infuriated him.

He'd fallen in love with the one woman who could never hear the persuasion techniques he'd spent a lifetime honing and perfecting, and she still considered him the greatest man to walk the earth. The day she was killed, Pierce vowed to develop a protocol to predict mass shootings. He'd feel like he was getting close to creating a viable system, and then an inexplicable detail would surface, adding more questions than answers.

"Pierce," Kelly whispered. Her head was tilted toward him with concern.

"Sorry, I'm fine," he replied, exhaling then inhaling deeply. It felt like he hadn't taken in a full breath for a while. The warm Texas breeze blew Kelly's hair into her face. Pierce turned to her and said, "Get us a vehicle. I'll brief you in the car."

"You got it, sir."

Kelly dipped her chin and, without hesitation, trotted to the valet stand in front of the hotel.

Pierce watched as Kelly placed a hand on the young valet's shoulder. Her technique was flawless. She used a standard confusion technique, with just enough physical movement to keep the man's eyes on her every move. Pierce listened in admiration. His methods hadn't been this polished so soon after his own graduation.

"I'm so sorry, but we aren't from here." She held her phone in front of the young man's face. "Which way exactly is northeast right now?"

Before the man could answer, she pointed south and continued. "You grew up here, I bet. Preschool here? You look so young and handsome—we're just...Jason! That's your name. So sorry." She touched him on the wrist.

"It's really so easy to notice when you don't have any attention now on what's not being right here in front of you," she motioned to the podium full of car keys, "and just ***become completely fine with it***...thank you so much for that—***you're happy to give that to me***," she touched her chest, "and it was the gray one there. That's completely fine, Jason. Thank you so much. I really appreciate it. That's the one right there. ***It's fine***."

To anyone listening, she sounded like an excited, rambling girl. To this man's brain, it was an avalanche of thick, heavy words that would soon fade into corners of his mind he couldn't reach.

The man passed her the keys to a vehicle, and she touched his forearm once more.

"Jason, it's fine—thank you. I was so discombobulated—things just ***spin around,*** and we ***forget now***...and then we all have those days...thinking ***nothing happened at all.***"

The young man's face was a blank canvas. She only did just enough to erase the emotional content of his memory. He nodded at her and his walkie-talkie began emitting chatter from the hotel staff. As his attention shifted, Kelly set an immediate course for the garage, Pierce following close behind. This woman was seriously impressive.

"How was that?" Kelly asked, cocking an eyebrow at him.

Pierce smiled. She made no effort to conceal her need for approval.

"Not too bad, Kelly. I'd like to play it down, but you've got some serious skills I don't see very often. Older siblings I imagine?"

"Three. Small house too." Kelly paused. "Pierce, I don't think that woman left her house of her own free will."

"I think you're correct. I found some scary—"

"There!"

Kelly pointed to a white sedan with flashing lights. She'd been clicking the vehicle's key to find its companion.

"I'll drive," Kelly said.

They climbed into the new Lexus. Kelly piloted the car through the back exit of the parking garage so as not to raise any concern at the valet counter.

"Where are we going?" Kelly asked, pulling the Lexus onto the freeway entrance road of Interstate 10.

"Can you just drive for a bit?"

Kelly nodded with concern.

Pierce stared off onto the freeway, wondering what his report to HIG should contain.

The day he had learned this at the HIG training compound in Yorktown, Alex Frost had been his instructor. Kelly had used a technique that was mild in comparison to what they had been taught to employ.

Initially, recruits went through a probation period—being observed on their 'off-time' without their knowledge to determine their level of integrity in the use of these techniques. Occasionally, someone would use them to commit a crime, mostly sexual assault or simple robbery. HIG taught a few simple but effective techniques the first week of class in order to expose the people who used them for personal gain or any reason that violated HIG policy governing the use of Tradecraft.

Pierce remembered learning to profile human weakness, fears, insecurities, and personality traits merely by looking at a person's appearance and outward behavior. This was the scariest part of the training. Initially, he thought he had been misreading everyone; they all looked secretly sad—afraid even. It wasn't until several weeks later that he learned this was the universal human condition: hiding flaws, wearing a mask, concealing fears, and posturing against our own weaknesses. It nearly crippled him to see the true nature of humans.

His cell phone brought him into the present moment, vibrating in his pocket.

‘Update HIG’ the message read.

"Have you been trained on phone protocol?" Pierce asked.

Kelly kept her eyes on the road and nodded. Pierce noticed her almost imperceptible smile.

"We're calling in now."

Pierce dialed a number from memory. The phone rang on speaker two times before a recorded voice answered.

"You're connected. Please go ahead."

The phone lines into HIG were monitored by humans, but they could never hear the operatives calling in. In the rare case an operative was captured or forced to call in to HIG, their influence skills would not be effective. Everything HIG operatives spoke into the phone was fed through a voice recognition software program and translated to a screen. The agents at HIG could respond with information or further directives using their own voice, but they could never hear the operatives they spoke to, only able to read their words on a screen.

"Poacher, Seven, Oxford," Pierce said.

His code words verified the line, and an operator responded with, "Thank you."

"Update to Houston. The woman, Miss Ferris, was likely kidnapped. Massive amounts of data sent to an unknown location from her personal computer. Possible private server in Europe. Files have been uploaded for your viewing. Looked like marketing research and video samples. Her alarm was disarmed from inside the house. Security system shows a woman named Catherine Norris. Police say she went to a comedy club just before coming to the victim's house, and she's a well-respected first-grade teacher. At the victim's desk were signs of tears around the keyboard. The woman cried, most likely while sending off her research. She also urinated in her office chair before leaving the house in her own vehicle with Miss Norris. She was terrified."

Kelly's mouth fell open.

The phone speakers crackled back to life with the soothing voice of the woman on the line. "Complete copy. Understand. What do you need?"

"Look up any similar incidents within the previous twenty-four hours."

Kelly took an exit Pierce guessed was in the direction of the Houston Airport.

The woman at HIG returned after a short pause.

"Confirmed two incidents. Similar circumstances. San Jose, California. Incident one was a twenty-three-year-old male working as a social media marketing consultant, and incident two was a thirty-four-year-old male employed at a high-end marketing firm working in the research department. They disappeared and incident response forensics discovered massive amounts of data transferred before their disappearance. Neither of them had packed bags, notified friends, or exhibited signs of a desire or intent to leave town according to the leading investigator's initial report. Please confirm this in San Jose. Waiting for updates."

"Copy. We will head to San Jose now."

"Thanks."

Pierce terminated the call.

Kelly glanced at him as she navigated a lane change. "What is this? Is this something that happens a lot? Dead marketing experts aren't really what we're in the business of pursuing. I don't even know what the hell I'm supposed to be doing. I'm not an investigator and we're chasing down some schoolteacher kidnapper like Dick Tracy. I'm in way over my head here."

Pierce gave her an understanding nod, holding up his palms. "I've got zero years of investigative work under my belt as well. I haven't had a chance to tell you about the blacklight. We've got two agents in Syria right now who do this kind of thing, but they're in the middle of persuading a group of Houthi rebels to destroy a stockpile of chemical weapons bound for Saudi Arabia at the moment. I don't know what the hell we're doing either. Let's just try and get to the bottom of it. For now, let's get to the plane and pour a drink. Sound good?"

Kelly nodded. Her lips tightened.

Withheld opinions.

Pierce continued. "And keep in mind...we're not chasing a kidnapper here. We're chasing a professional. I'm not trying to scare you, but if you treat a lion like a housecat, you're a lot more likely to get torn to pieces."

Kelly took a breath and nodded. She ran her fingers through her hair. "Let's get to San Jose."

CHAPTER 15
SAN JOSE, CALIFORNIA

Trent broke the trust of the man he feared most by watching a video.

What he'd learned was so fascinating that he didn't mind much. He still got his assignments done; it was just a lot easier when he could get someone else to do it. His face would never be on video, and he'd never be tied back to a single eyewitness account of the incident.

In the video he saw back in Budapest, Trent learned a strange phrase consisting of twelve words. He didn't understand it until the video explained the proper use of the technique. The evening he discovered it was the night all his beliefs about human beings were shaken to the core.

Trent had visited the magnificent pool in the Hotel Stacio near the Budapest Airport the evening he learned the phrase. The pool area was opulent with blue tiles plating most of the room, low ceilings, and dim lighting, making it look like some Roman king's private pool. The smell of chlorine always reminded him of his military training.

A slim, long legged woman placed a magazine on a lounger near Trent and he'd noticed immediately that it was printed in English.

After a brief conversation, Trent whispered the phrase to her and watched her intently for some kind of reaction.

Initially, she only blinked a few times, but then she turned into something resembling a zombie on her lounger–staring at him with eyes that didn't blink. He'd thought he had paralyzed her; he immediately told her to sit up, and she did without a moment's hesitation. In fact, he discovered she did anything he commanded. That evening, Trent told her he was her husband.

*****

The phrase didn't work on everyone. He tried it on several people, and many of them just looked at him like he was speaking another language. Trent became obsessed with discovering how it worked and scoured the internet for any information on how the brain worked and responded to words. After seeing the word hypnosis multiple times, he decided that *might* be what the phrase was. Hypnosis. Some kind of hypnosis bullshit. It didn't last long unless he repeated the phrase every hour or so. People would just snap out of it unless he stayed with them and continued to say it.

On the flight to Houston, Trent read all about it. He still understood very little. He looked up local hypnotists in hopes of finding an answer to why the phrase only worked about a third of the time. He ran across an ad for a hypnosis show at a Houston comedy club and bought a ticket with cash at the door.

That evening, he learned everything he needed to know.

A hypnotist named Rich Mars was performing. During the show, Trent watched as the hypnotist asked the audience to close their eyes and hold out their hands. Once they complied, the hypnotist began suggesting things, like that they were holding something heavy in one hand and something much lighter in the other hand. Trent watched in amazement as the more suggestible people lowered one hand and raised the other hand, placing a target on themselves to be picked for the show.

Another trick the hypnotist performed was convincing people that their hands were stuck together. There were people in the audience who could not unstick their hands until Rich told them they were unstuck. Trent was fascinated.

The people acted like idiots; the crowd was pleased.

After the show, Trent approached the hypnotist. Rich had set up a table near the bar to sell DVDs of the performance. He introduced himself as Jakey.

People lined up to ask Rich questions and buy videos of their friends acting like idiots on stage. But Trent managed to get to the side of the table next to Rich, and, in between selling his merchandise, Trent was able to ask Rich the questions he needed.

"How come it doesn't work on everyone in the room?" Trent asked over the bar music.

"It's a numbers game. Anyone can be hypnotized, but it's just a matter of time. When you only have a few minutes, the ones that are the most suggestible are the ones you need to work with."

Trent had told him he was an aspiring stage hypnotist, which somehow made the man reveal all kinds of stuff Trent assumed were supposed to be trade secrets.

"So, suggestibility is what you have to look for?" Trent asked.

"Yeah. It's super easy. Whoever responds more to the suggestions in the beginning are the ones we work with most of the time."

The crowd of people at the table began to dissipate. Trent kept an eye on his target—the younger woman who had responded dramatically to all the hypnosis stuff in the show.

He turned back to Rich and said, "So, how do you identify suggestible people if you're *not* doing all the tests?"

Trent could tell he was pressing this man's time. Rich stepped away from Trent to take another person's credit card before saying, "Look, man, come to a few more shows. You'll see it. They all have smooth skin under their eyes."

"Smooth skin?"

"Yeah. Like, they don't have wrinkles in the skin just below the eye. Smooth like a baby's butt. Most of the time, you could talk them into anything if you know what you're doing."

Trent thanked the man, promising he would attend his future shows. He wouldn't.

Just outside of the comedy club in Houston, the last of the people filtered out of the now-closing bar. Trent approached the dark-haired, suggestible woman he'd seen on stage earlier. He had spent the evening watching her respond with enthusiasm to all the suggestibility tests that Rich used on the audience.

Trent eyed her from a safe distance. Her legs were a chiseled work of art and her face was the kind that made men stealthily remove wedding rings. As she hugged her friends goodbye and walked to her car alone, he spoke the phrase to her and watched with elation as she instantly stumbled into a nearby wall of a parking garage. She picked herself up and stared at him as a child would stare into the eyes of a parent—waiting for approval, permission, a command of some sort. The skin under her eyes was *exactly* as Rich described.

He knew he could simply use her to get his assignment done—heading to some marketing executive's home and getting the woman to send the research to Aphid. She could even get rid of the woman if he could somehow make her forget everything. He could just tell her to erase it from her mind like the hypnotist did when he made someone forget the number seven.

He told her to pull out her phone. She did.

"Look at me."

She peered up at him with an innocence that almost made him regret his choice to use her.

"Type the following message into your social newsfeed."

She nodded.

"Taking a break from social media for a while."

She posted it to three different social media accounts. Notifications began rolling in from concerned friends. Trent ignored them as he powered her phone down.

*****

San Jose had comedy hypnosis shows too.

They weren't exactly like the ones in Houston, but Trent could see the similarities: testing for suggestible people, pulling them onstage, and weeding out the ones who didn't go all the way into a trance as the show progressed. He quite preferred this method to get his work done. His hands stayed clean. The people would never remember him. He had even developed a protocol for selecting his 'workers.'

Go to the show.

Find someone with a small number of friends.

Identify who responds best to the suggestibility tests.

Find them after the show.

Get them alone.

Have them collect the marketing research and kill the target.

Get out clean.

Tonight, the show featured a comedy hypnotist who went through the same process Rich Mars had.

Rich had told him that hypnotists also weed out people who were 'super suggestible' in the beginning. If they fell to the floor when they were told to 'sleep,' they were called 'floppers.'

Floppers had become Trent's favorite people to influence. It required almost no effort to isolate them after the show, and they were shockingly obedient, practically becoming blank slates once he spoke the special phrase.

The waiter brought his food to the table. These clubs didn't like empty space, so he'd been placed at a table with a young couple who doted on each other and still held hands. Clearly newlyweds.

"You come here alone?" the man across the small table asked him.

"Well, I didn't intend to. Last-minute argument with the wife, and I didn't want to waste the ticket. Non-refundable. Ryan Moss," Trent said, extending his hand across the table. The couple introduced themselves, but he couldn't care less about their names. Years of special operations training had taught him to be 'more forgettable than likable' so he could slip out after the show and find his target.

As the meal came to a close, Trent learned the couple had recently returned from a trip to India. They wanted to tell anyone they could about how enlightened they had become after they toured the yoga and meditation gurus along India's west coast. Trent nodded intermittently and uttered an occasional 'wow.'

The lights in the room dimmed as the stage lights lit up. The comedy club looked like a typical restaurant but was a little cramped. It was decorated to look nice—dark green carpets and white tablecloths—but the stench of spilled beer lingered in the air. A hundred people seemed to be content with the place, however, as their attention narrowed to the main stage.

The DJ introduced the hypnotist, Terry Kindle, and the crowd clapped him onto the small stage at the front of the room.

Terry came onto the stage gripping a microphone and began his opener. It sounded a lot like Rich's opening speech, explaining how hypnosis works and alleviating the audience of fears caused by bad press, movies, and sci-fi films.

"...and you can't get stuck in hypnosis. If I hypnotize you and leave the room, you'll come out like you took a fabulous nap," Terry continued.

He began the suggestibility testing. People clasped their hands together and Terry suggested they were 'locked tight' and the audience couldn't open their hands no matter how hard they tried.

Trent watched as a few guys pulled their hands apart, shrugging to their girlfriends like it was no big deal.

Douchebags.

As the testing continued, Terry's big-breasted assistant began walking the highly suggestible people to the stage.

"...and I want you to imagine in your left hand there's a massive pile of books. With each passing second, the books become heavier and heavier. Heavier and heavier still as the seconds pass. And that right arm. Imagine I've tied a hundred massive helium balloons to your wrist. Pulling up. *Harder and harder.* Just pulling that right arm right up into the air with more and more force. And noticing those books in the left hand becoming even heavier. That's right..."

Trent looked on as the members of the audience participated in the spectacle.

A young woman in the front row responded exceptionally well to the suggestions. The hypnotist's assistant calmly walked over to her and bent down to whisper in her ear. The woman stood, with help from the assistant, and was ushered onstage with the other suggestible responders.

As the hypnotist continued his act and transitioned into putting the people onstage to 'sleep,' he told them to stare at the stage lights as he spoke.

He spoke into the microphone in a slow, deep, but commanding voice as he described the process of descending a staircase, counting down from ten to one.

"...EIGHT. Your muscles becoming loose and limp like a rag doll. Everything completely unwinding and letting loose. Letting go.

"SEVEN. All the way down. Those tiny muscles around the eyes letting go, relaxing into places you've never really relaxed before.

"SIX. Completely limp and loose like a ragdoll. That's right. Allllllllll the way down..."

The young woman Trent had been eyeing sat near center stage. She had smooth skin under her eyes too. As the hypnotist said the word 'FIVE,' she slumped in her chair a bit and then fell completely onto the stage floor, motionless.

A flopper. This shit actually works. She's the one.

The assistant helped the woman back to her seat. Rich told Trent they didn't like the floppers because, while they might be highly suggestible, they tend to do just that—flop. In a comedy show, they didn't make great candidates for an exciting performance.

Trent watched her continue to respond to the commands for the rest of the show. Even sitting at her table with a friend, she responded like the champion suggestible subject she was. It was truly beautiful for Trent to witness.

After the show, Terry Kindle sold paraphernalia outside near the exit, as Rich Mars had in Houston.

At the bar, Trent saw her. She was muscular. Pretty. She had only come with one friend who was hugging her goodnight. Her friend kissed her cheek and walked out of the front exit of the comedy club.

Trent made his way over to the woman and struck up a quick conversation.

"Wow. That whole thing was amazing. I was upset they pulled you off the stage."

She turned to Trent with a smile. "I know! I still felt like I was in the show somehow. I really liked it."

Trent agreed and introduced himself as Peter Thomas.

She extended a hand. "Nicole. Glad to meet you, Peter."

"You look like a dancer or something."

"Yoga instructor, actually." Her eyebrows shot upward in excitement. "I've got a studio just a couple blocks from here. You should stop by sometime! My website is yogaandwine.org. You should totally check it out. I'm just headed out to meet my ride outside."

"Me too. I'm meeting my wife outside. You still did an awesome job!"

Trent knew mentioning a wife would eliminate any suspicions she had of his intentions. As predicted, she accompanied him out of the club. Trent discussed his prior issues with drinking, only to ensure he spoke the phrase 'no more alcohol' loud enough for the security guys at the front door to hear, hoping that if they saw Trent helping her walk, they would assume she was drunk.

In the dark parking lot, he pretended to search for a car. Five minutes prior, he had activated the battery-powered eight-antenna jammer in his small bag, ensuring no one near him could use an electronic device. A necessary precaution for two reasons: For one, if something went wrong, he would have time to escape before anyone could snap a photo, or otherwise incriminate him. The second reason being if the phrase didn't work on Nicole, and she decided to call the police, she couldn't.

It's now or never.

"Nicole!"

She spun to face him. He placed a gentle hand on her shoulder, reciting the phrase he'd spent nights memorizing. Her eyes instantly glazed over. Her legs shifted beneath her. Her body leaned forward, and Trent saw the security guards glance over without concern.

"We're going to get in this black BMW right there. I've got someone to drive us. There's a really special project I have for you."

She nodded.

Another clean assignment.

CHAPTER 16

YORKTOWN, VIRGINIA

Deidra Collins was exhausted. After having agents run down potential leaks, and coming up with little to no evidence, Deidra initiated a cleanup plan. The teams in each location were to scrub hard drives, swap every piece of electronics, vehicles, and, in some cases, would leave their assigned country altogether.

HIG operatives were always monitored closely when carrying anything electronic that contained sensitive HIG data.

Deidra sat in her office and stared aimlessly at her bookshelf. It was sparse but still had a woman's touch, at least she thought. After graduating from the Naval Academy and leaving the Navy as a Commander, she felt like she had lost part of her feminine side. The office smelled like lavender—like a spa. She liked that. Her massive oak bookshelf contained the works of the men and women who began and grew HIG into the silent global leader it was today. Thomas Paine, Benjamin Franklin, and even the rare book titled *Mental Medicine*.

Deidra's desk phone rang, pulling her out of her thoughts. She picked up the black, shiny handset and pressed it to her ear.

"Go." She spoke sharply.

"Ma'am, it's Evan. I've just finished our sweep of the entire system and file logs of every device belonging to our members. We have a red flag."

"Red flag?" Deidra sat upright in her chair and leaned into the desk.

"Yes ma'am. It was a video file transferred off of a HIG iPad."

"Evan, I can't do this one piece at a time. Give me everything."

"Sorry. Yes. The HIG iPad was compromised in the main terminal of the new Istanbul airport. We don't know who has the data. From what I can piece together, there were USB charging stations in the private meeting rooms inside of the Turkish Airlines lounge. One of our agents plugged in the iPad and it wasn't just a charger. It hacked the iPad for a specific file with a query for the filename. It didn't transfer anything else. If it wasn't the charger, it was the cable provided by the lounge. Those cables can have a small computer in what you *think* is a normal USB plug. The file uploaded to a server in Budapest and that's the last place we've seen it."

Deidra took a slow, collected breath. "Evan, I need the filename now. And a name."

"Yes—the file was—*is* called 'P7 Manners.' Phrase Seven. It's the file the hacking system looked for *specifically*. If it hits a network, I can see where it is; I can track it. Like, if someone who's online opens or uses the file."

Deidra didn't necessarily feel her pulse quicken in times like this, but her heart seemed to pound at her ribcage much harder.

"Who was it, Evan?"

"It was one of ours. The iPad is still intact and in our possession."

"Evan, last chance."

"Mr. Reston." His voice cracked.

"Pierce?" Deidra's jaw muscles tightened.

"Yes, ma'am."

"Find the goddamn video, Evan. And thank you for the report."

She hung up the phone with a loud *smack!* and snatched a pencil from her drawer. Let out a calm, controlled breath while writing down the details of the report onto a small notecard.

She pulled out her phone and set in motion the protocol for a missing HIG phrase. Within minutes, everyone would be looking for the man who had it, and there wasn't a human immune to the reach and persuasion of HIG.

Deidra looked out onto the sprawling green lawn. It had been seven months since Pierce had been in Istanbul. Whoever took this thing from his iPad either hadn't figured out how to decode it or had simply decided not to use it.

But a third option made her stop breathing. She had to hold the desk to steady herself.

If whoever took it knew how to employ it on a massive scale, it could be far worse than a nuclear weapon.

CHAPTER 17 SAN JOSE, CALIFORNIA

"Mind control is pretty easy. All the ingredients are always there, it's just that people don't have the recipe." Pierce felt the landing gear lowering and tightened his seatbelt.

"Who do you think is doing this?" Kelly prodded.

"I don't know. We're damn sure going to find out."

The Gulfstream GV Jet bounced onto the runway at the San Jose International Airport and waited in line behind several larger commercial jets to taxi to a private hangar beside the main airport.

As Pierce's phone connected to the local network, it began ringing. It was a Houston area code.

A Houston Police Officer provided Pierce with the contact information for a Mr. Rich Mars, the stage hypnotist who performed at the show before the marketing woman went missing. Pierce remembered the officer had a tattoo on his forearm of a police flag. In small letters under the flag had been the words 'FIRST RESPONDER / FIRST LINE.'

Need for recognition and approval. Strong sense of duty. Responsive to flattery.

Pierce listened carefully to the young man, jotted the contact information down, and thanked him.

"Officer Brooks, I'm really thankful we have people like you in Houston. I can't imagine working as hard as you guys do with all the manning shortfalls. Thanks very much."

He could almost hear the serotonin now pumping into the young officer's brain.

After the brief call, Pierce stood in the aisle of the taxiing plane. Kelly peered up at him.

"Hypnotist guy?" she asked.

"Yep. Want to talk to him?"

"Hell yes. Do you think he's involved?" Kelly's eyes widened and her hands curled into fists.

Pierce smiled. "I doubt it, but we need to see if he saw anything unusual the night the marketing woman went missing in Houston."

"Why would a hypnotist be involved?" Kelly's face scrunched up as she pondered the reason.

Pierce shook his head.

"I don't know. A lot of people think hypnosis is pretty dangerous. There's even been people arrested for using it to commit crimes. What we do involves a tiny bit of that artform, but it's still vastly different from hypnosis. Hypnosis is, for the most part, consensual, whereas *we* hijack the brain. I'm still not sure what possible connection there is. When you learned hypnosis at HIG, I bet it *initially* seemed like a cool technique."

"Yeah. I thought it was incredible."

"Right. But after you learned the HIG techniques, everything changed. That's why so many people confuse hypnosis with a lot of the mind control stuff online."

"I'll call him now. You should speak to him; see what he knows."

Pierce looked back and forth between a notecard and his phone while he punched in numbers and handed the phone to Kelly on speaker.

A man with a New York accent answered the phone.

"Mr. Mars?" Kelly confirmed

"Yeah, who's this?"

Kelly glanced at Pierce. "Sir, this is Special Investigator Holly Thompson. I know you've already spoken to the Houston Police Department; I also know you're a very busy man. Thank you so much for taking my call."

"Yeah. Of course. No worries. Call me Rich. What can I do for you, Miss Holly?"

Kelly continued, "Well, I'm looking at this case file here, and I was wondering if you saw the woman who disappeared from the club the night of the show."

"I did. She was in the crowd. Had a friend with her as I recall. Nice lady. Looked rich, but she didn't come onstage or anything like that. Just watched. She looked like she had a good time at the show. I didn't see anything unusual about her if that's what you're asking, but I already told the other cops that."

"I also wanted to know if there was anything you noticed at all about the entire night that might have stood out to you. Something that comes to mind that seemed out of the ordinary or unusual..."

"Nah. Not really. The show was the same as any other night."

"Thanks, Rich. Appreciate that. I know you're busy, but could you just walk me through the night so I can just kind of get a feel for it?"

Pierce leaned in, closing his eyes and waiting for the response.

"Yeah! Of course. No worries. We start the show with some basic explanations of hypnosis, so people aren't scared of it. Dispel some misconceptions people might have and test the audience to see who in the audience is going to be the best to work with."

The plane turned to the right, pulling into the San Jose Net Jet hangar.

Rich continued, "After that, we picked people who were good subjects and pulled them up onstage. They go through what's called an induction after that."

"An induction?" Kelly interrupted. Even though she had been trained in advanced hypnosis.

"Yeah. Sorry. An induction is where you hypnotize someone for real–they go into trance and you make 'em do stuff on the stage. We go through that bit, do a bunch of funny routines, and at the end of the show, I give everyone a chance to get some of the real benefits of hypnosis–just, like, suggestions for motivation, discipline, positivity, and that stuff. People love it."

"Fascinating," Kelly said. "What happens after the show?

Rich paused for a second. "Every place is different. But in Houston, we'll wrap the show, and my assistant and I meet the guests in the bar on the way out. They can buy merchandise, DVD's, signed pictures, and audio tapes for personal improvement. Really good stuff."

"Great. Thanks. Is that all that happened in your memory of the show in Houston?" Kelly asked.

"Far as I know. I mean, we have groupies; there was a new groupie in training that night. It's not, like, a bunch of hot chicks, either. We're talkin' about strange guys who just love hypnosis and somehow attach to me. They fly around the country and come to almost all my shows."

Kelly laughed.

"I'm serious, Holly. It's not glamorous at all. That night we had a new one. They come up after the show and ask all kinds of questions about hypnosis and mind control and shit. Usually, they're a little bit off—socially. This guy in Houston comes up after the show—they never almost never buy anything—he basically wants to know all about hypnosis and how it works and how many people it can be used on."

"Got it. Are any of those questions unusual for the groupies?"

"Nah. Not really. But he did ask about safety. No one ever gives a shit about that when they start."

"Like, what kind of safety?"

"I don't totally remember now, but it was something about people falling when they get hypnotized."

"Great. Thank you. Remember what he looked like?"

"Yeah. The police already asked me, but he was, like, maybe five-nine. White guy. Big ass brown beard. Fit looking. Athlete, maybe. I don't think I got his name. If I did, I don't remember, but he did have on a *weird* scarf. It looked like one of those Muslim scarfs."

"A shemagh?"

"I guess, if that's what they call it. One of the ones the guys wear over there on their head. But it was almost like a mix between gray and tan, and it had tiny fish scales on it—or something that looked like fish scales."

"Like sequins?"

"No. I don't know how to describe it. It was like super tiny fish scales."

"Okay. Thank you so much, Rich. Please save my number if you start to realize you can *remember more*, or when you think of anything else. You can call me any time."

"You bet. No problem. Take care."

Pierce's jaw tightened into a rock. He opened his eyes and straightened up. "That was a professional. He's able to appear submissive and insecure around someone used to being fawned over after a show, and he knew to wear a shimmer scarf for the cameras."

"What the hell is a 'shimmer scarf?' Sounds like something you'd see in a women's store," Kelly asked.

"It's essentially a huge light amplifier. Underneath it, there are hundreds of infrared LED lights, totally invisible to the human eye. The scarf magnifies them through what he called fish scales. Those little reflect the light and basically blind any security camera. The different color changes on the scarf look random to us but they all resemble parts of human faces for facial recognition cameras. The camera sees not just the blurry face, but a jumbled mess of *other* facial features. That scarf basically makes cameras completely ignore the entire image."

"Whoa."

"Yeah. They cost around five thousand dollars and they're *not* easy to find."

Kelly took in a breath and nodded absently. "Professional."

As the pilot opened the plane's door, Kelly pulled out her 'go bag'.

Pierce opened his kit and withdrew two FN Five-seveN pistols, six twenty-round magazines, and two holsters. He slammed a magazine into the gun and chambered a round.

He handed a loaded, holstered pistol to Kelly.

"If this is a professional, we need to be prepared for things nine millimeters can't penetrate."

The Five-seveN handgun was capable of firing small rifle ammunition that could penetrate standard body armor and carried twenty rounds in a lightweight magazine.

One of the pilots leaned into the cabin from the doorway. "We've got a vehicle here for you guys," he said as he lowered the stairs onto the slick floor of the hangar.

"We will be here on standby until we hear from you. We'll stay with the plane."

The pilot handed a set of Ford keys to Pierce. "Should be parked just outside the hangar. Ford Explorer. Black."

"Thanks, Tim." Pierce took the keys and shook the pilot's hand.

Kelly and Pierce descended the stairs with their bags and walked out of the hangar into the bright California sun.

In California, there was one profession that allowed you to speed at will and drive like an emergency vehicle: a contract firefighter. During the summer months, and well into the fall, firefighters would take on temporary jobs to strap on loads of safety gear and race into the forests at the earliest hint of a fire. They weren't city firefighters, and they didn't have uniforms, but they enjoyed many of the freedoms a regular city firefighter would when it came to traffic violations. The cover identities would also help to explain the unusual equipment they had, as well as the lack of local identification.

Pierce tossed the keys to Kelly. She clicked the 'lock' button until the horn sounded on a nearby Ford Explorer. They loaded the bags into the back of the vehicle and drove out of the airport parking through a private security gate for the local VIPs.

"Where to?" Kelly said as she touched the navigation screen on the vehicle.

"Don't use the vehicle GPS, it will stay in its memory. Use your HIG phone. Let's get to the comedy club and get whatever video we can on this."

Kelly punched in the address on her phone and they sped toward the comedy club.

Pierce's phone rang again. It was Deidra. He answered the call on speakerphone.

"Hey, Deidra. What's up?"

"How are things in California?"

"Just landed. We're heading to the comedy club now to see if we can get video. Police reports say they found the same thing we did in Houston. Teardrops near the computer keyboard for the missing marketing guy. Forced to email research."

"The uploads of all the marketing data are going to an IP address in the Czech Republic," Deidra said. "We can't let this get out of control, Pierce. Are you driving?"

"No, ma'am. Kelly is."

Deidra let out a sigh. "Guys. We have a leak. A phrase training video was stolen from a HIG tablet. It was Phrase Seven."

Pierce's heart hammered in his chest. He shook his head in disbelief. For almost four hundred years HIG had kept its secrets hidden from public view.

"Who the hell compromised us, Deidra?" Pierce asked. His grip constricted around the phone.

"The video was taken from *your* iPad, Pierce. Phrase Seven has been in the open for almost *seven months.* It was taken off your iPad in an airport lounge in Istanbul. Through a public charging outlet."

Pierce's head spun. "There's no fucking way," he snapped. His blood boiled.

"Pierce, the *entire* digital team here has been through the data."

His body was warm, and his stomach pulled hard toward the earth. He had compromised HIG. This was his fault. While serving as the senior operations officer, he had single-handedly compromised HIG.

Whatever degree of death that followed was his doing. *His* fault.

CHAPTER 18
PRAGUE, CZECH REPUBLIC

Dimitri saw many things in his life, but the rows of comatose women in hospital beds before him was by far the strangest.

He stood on a metal walkway, part of an upper platform overlooking the most modern medical facility he'd seen in his life. It had been built by Aphid inside of a dusty, abandoned-looking warehouse. Aphid had constructed a modern building inside of the old warehouse that Dimitri thought was the cleanest and most well-decorated facility he had ever seen.

The lights were dimmed to the point of darkness, except for the lower-level medical rooms Aphid had built in the center of the first floor. Looking down into the medical bay, he counted forty-one rooms, all containing motionless people in hospital beds. The ceilings of each hospital room were glass and allowed light to escape into the upper level of the warehouse. Each room had a large television hung on the wall that tilted toward the hospital beds.

As a visual and graphic designer, Aphid brought Dimitri into the fold to help build a video that Aphid described as *world-changing.* Dimitri didn't see why; it was basically a clickbait video that had weird words in it and talked about suicide statistics. Aphid firmly insisted the video be made utilizing the hundreds of marketing research papers written in English Aphid had given him. He thought it was stupid, but for ninety-five thousand euros, he was fine doing a few days' worth of work.

Today Aphid would test his video. Aphid *himself* had asked for Dimitri by name to be present for the test. It made him walk taller. Aphid had only spoken to him once, but it was like talking to a man who could see you naked, knew every bad thing you had ever done, and still treated you with respect and courtesy.

Dimitri had no idea what the video was for. He watched it and thought it was quite stupid. His trust, however, was not in the job, but in Aphid.

After two days in the warehouse, Dimitri had completed every task Aphid asked of him, and his work was finished. Aphid, being a noble man, invited him up to the overwatch level to observe some sort of medical demonstration on the sick people below.

When Dimitri first met Aphid in Ukraine, he was working as a marketing consultant for one of Aphid's wealthy friends. Aphid possessed a candor and presence that captivated him. It seemed to enchant anyone Aphid spoke to. At only 5'6," Aphid commanded the presence of a supernatural giant and was kind to everyone he met. He was as close to a god as Dimitri had ever seen. His face looked like it had been worn by years of hard work and sacrifice. His gray hair seemed like a crown of glory. Aphid spoke slowly, and with such conviction, his raspy voice only seemed to enhance his natural authority.

Dimitri was most entertained by the amount of money Aphid paid everyone. What a wonderful man to take such good care of the people in his charge. He truly understood the struggle of ordinary life and wanted others to succeed.

Dimitri had worked hard to ensure his work was commensurate with the money he had received. He could live for two or three years on the single duffel bag of cash Aphid had graciously provided him.

His work on the video was extremely specific. Documents written in American English were posted to a hard drive and he was to implement every piece of research in the video.

Aphid provided him with over sixty thousand pages of research. Dimitri struggled to incorporate everything into a short, forty-second video, but he managed. The research he had been going through was groundbreaking work, revealing the exact methods to build a video that could instantly capture and hold the attention of anyone scrolling through a social media news feed. The trouble with online videos was that the volume didn't always play automatically, and you had to further convince the person watching to activate the sound on their device so they could hear it. This is where the second half of the research he had been handed came into play. He had dissected the confidential research to ensure the video *fully* achieved every aspect of what the paper's American writers called 'attentional captivity'.

Dimitri was genuinely shocked by how well the video came out. Despite being forced to produce it in a locked room and being unable to show a single person to get feedback, he was still proud. He hadn't seen Aphid during his trip, but he understood Aphid was a busy man. Dimitri assumed the video must be a suicide prevention campaign.

He peered down onto two long rows of hospital rooms below with their glass ceilings sending light into the dark upper level of the warehouse. The people in the comas started to move. Small movements at first. Dimitri couldn't tell, but it seemed like they were all waking up at the same time. He leaned forward, straining to see if the patients' eyes were opening, but couldn't make them out.

A steel door opening from behind startled him, and he turned to see the man he admired so much emerge from the dark hallway behind the door. Aphid appeared, wearing a suit that looked as trim and neat as the one he'd seen him wear in Ukraine when they had met. Dimitri couldn't find a single thing wrong with the man.

Everything about this man is admirable.

Just behind Aphid was a tall man in a lab coat with perfectly combed, short black hair. They stepped onto the metal platform and Aphid extended his arms like a father coming home to a child. Dimitri didn't miss a beat and stepped over to the man, hugging him tightly. The man in the lab coat extended a hand to Dimitri.

"Please, call me Nick."

"Glad to meet you, sir." Dimitri smiled nervously, bewildered and confused as to what all was happening.

"He's our head physician here, Dimitri," Aphid said. "You look very well. Thank you for coming to our rescue when we needed you most. All of us are very grateful to you."

"Sir, I am glad to work with you anytime. I would love a chance to work with you whenever there is—"

A loud beep echoed through the warehouse from below. Dimitri's gaze shifted down to the massive medical facility.

"Are we ready?" Aphid said, eyes locked on his creation.

The doctor tapped on his phone and gave a cursory nod. "We can start in about one minute, sir. They got the injections about two minutes ago and should all be awake soon."

"Perfect. Thank you, Doctor. Dimitri, you've given us the means to correct so many problems in this world. I used the same phrase from the video on you the day you arrived to begin your work. I was so pleased to see you are immune to it. You proved your worth beyond what I've paid you. This event is historic. It marks a turning point for all of us and will lead a new path to human understanding and compassion."

"Thank you, Aphid, sir. I am honored. What do you mean immune to the phrase? It's only a string of words."

Ignoring his question, Aphid turned to the doctor. "Are we ready?"

The doctor nodded.

"Let's do it," Aphid commanded.

The doctor pulled a small, handheld walkie-talkie from his lab coat pocket and said in Czech to the men in masks below, "*Zbraně.*" *Weapons.*

Aphid had hired only non-English-speaking people to run the operation in the warehouse, with Dimitri being the only exception. Aphid had told him it was for safety, but he didn't know why.

Aphid and the doctor turned and stepped to the guard rail to gaze down into the glass-topped rooms below.

Four men in black face masks were going room to room. Dimitri stepped to the guard rail and observed alongside the two other men. What he saw sent a cold chill through his entire body. Something wasn't right.

The masked men each held rectangular cardboard boxes. As they entered each room, they produced a black handgun and placed them gently on the bedside table next to the patients.

Dimitri glanced at Aphid and the doctor, hoping to see some indication that they didn't agree with this. They gave away nothing. They continued intently watching the action below, so Dimitri followed suit. He leaned onto the railing and tried as hard as he could to suppress his growing sense of discomfort.

The men completed placing black handguns on the bedside table of every occupant in the medical facility and walked to the end of the glass-covered hallway.

The doctor once again spoke into the walkie-talkie. "*Spust'te video.*" *Start the video.*

When he finished, the men below reached back into the cardboard boxes and each produced a set of over-the-ear hearing protection and lowered them over their ears.

Aphid leaned slightly toward Dimitri. "Safety precaution."

The lights dimmed in every room, and the light from the large televisions in each room glowed as if they were all just turned on.

"Your video will make a new way forward for humanity, Dimitri. I'm proud of you."

The words from Aphid, even amidst the strange happenings below, somehow made Dimitri surge with pride and excitement.

The televisions in each room flickered to life, and flashes from the screens reflected onto their white walls.

It was his video. The small, short flashes were designed to interrupt the pattern-behavior of scrolling through social media. It was one of the many mandatory inclusions based on the American research that Aphid provided.

The flashes were the first part of the video. They only flashed for a moment—enough to get the attention of the social media user. Dimitri turned to see Aphid and the doctor placing black hearing protection over their ears. Dimitri's confusion deepened, but he couldn't pull himself away from the events unfolding below.

The video progressed, and every patient in the rooms entirely captivated by it. Dimitri struggled to hear the audio well enough to make out the words, but he knew the words. He knew the whole video.

As the video came to an end, he looked to Aphid and the doctor, bewildered.

"Mister Aphid, I–"

Aphid held up a sharp hand, keeping his eyes on the facility below.

Dimitri surrendered to the two men's focus on the patients below and continued observing. It was strange. Most sat still, transfixed on the televisions that had all been shut off.

In the closest room to him was a blonde woman. Dimitri watched as she glanced around the room, spotted the gun, and seized it.

These people are going to hurt each other.

Dimitri started to back away, and felt Aphid's calm, yet firm, grip on his forearm. He looked back. Most of the patients were now holding guns. He heard a pop that made him jump at first, then dove to the ground.

These people are shooting at us!

He continued hearing gunfire and leaned over to see what was happening. Some patients were slumped in their beds, the white walls splattered with blood, while other patients had fallen to the floor. They had shot themselves in the head.

Two were still alive. They didn't shoot themselves at all. They didn't even pick up the gun.

Dimitri struggled to breathe. His chest tightened and a nameless dread engulfed him.

He laid on his side on the metal walkway. Aphid knelt and placed a gentle hand on his shoulder. "You did a wonderful job, Dimitri. You've provided this world a way out of certain chaos and destruction, and you've made good on every promise. Your family will be taken care of."

Dimitri took a moment to process everything Aphid said, and finally recoiled in fear as Aphid produced a small, silenced pistol.

"No! No! I am okay! I'm going to keep secrets. It's okay. I promise I'm going to—"

Aphid pushed Dimitri's forehead backward with the end of the silencer and fired a single shot.

CHAPTER 19
SAN JOSE, CALIFORNIA

Pierce couldn't shake the feeling of responsibility. There were strict protocols at HIG. One of them was never to plug electronics into public charging outlets.

He didn't know what to say to Alex, the man who had made him who he was. His personal mentor.

Pierce and Kelly checked into the Hotel Valencia in San Jose and sat at a table in the center outdoor courtyard of the hotel. A large, long infinity fountain ran down the center of the courtyard dining area bubbled along with the occasional sound of silverware and conversation. The atmosphere did nothing for Pierce's sense of guilt. Kelly had been talking to him for nearly an hour and Pierce had barely heard her.

The waiter delivered his second gin and tonic to the table. Pierce took in a long, slow breath and looked at Kelly with vivid determination.

"What's next?" She asked.

"We need to get ahold of the witnesses. There's a lot we don't know, but we need a description of this guy. If there was someone who saw him, we need to talk to them."

Kelly sat upright in her seat at the table, almost knocking over her wine glass. "Pierce, look at me."

Pierce turned and looked her in the eye. Her eyebrows rose slightly, telling him she was surprised he'd done as she asked.

"We don't know how long we have, or even if there is a connection here, but we need to act now. You're responsible. Get over it. Everyone fucks up. I just emailed Deidra to see if there are any updates."

Pierce looked at her, realizing why she was so good at the job despite being so new. She had no reservations, ever. Not that she lacked candor or tact, just that Kelly didn't worry herself about anything. She was never in her own head in a conversation. Pierce would pay for that kind of clarity.

He placed a hand on Kelly's knee. "I'm going to call Alex."

Kelly looked at Pierce with tightened lips and sympathetic eyes and nodded. Pierce pulled out a phone and stood. He dialed Alex as he walked away; before the second ring, Alex answered.

"Pierce, don't say a goddamn word. We all make mistakes. If you're sitting there in self-loathing, and I know *for a fact* you're drinking, you need to stop now. Not only do you need to set an example for that young lady, but you also need to figure out what's going on and put yourself and Kelly well in front of it. Say yes if you got all that."

Pierce uttered a reluctant 'yes'.

"Good. Next: no doubt you've assumed full personal responsibility for this. Everyone makes small choices, and everyone makes mistakes. If you're assuming all the blame for whatever this is, you're a narcissist. Only a narcissist would think they have full control over the world, and that you're sitting at the center of the issue without anyone else. If this is the case, stop it. You're not a narcissist, and you've got a job to do. Aristotle said it best when he talked about character being the most effective means of persuasion. I need you now, and so do a lot of people! Go find out who the hell is behind this. I'm sending you three images taken from people at the comedy club there in San Jose. We have our guy. Pour out whatever shit you're drinking and go find him."

"Alex, thank y—"

"You're welcome. Don't let a bad situation ruin good character."

The phone beeped and the line went dead. Pierce took a moment to center himself and walked back to Kelly at the table.

"Ready?" he asked Kelly.

She beamed in response as she yanked a hundred-dollar bill from her small purse and tossed it onto the table. Pierce took a final sip from his gin and tonic and poured it out into a potted plant.

"We have photos of the guy. Looks like the guy Rich described from the hypnosis show in

Houston. We need to get into the San Jose Police Department and get video of all the traffic cams coming in and out of the club. We can track this moron down a lot faster with a description and some photos, hopefully within the hour. I'm assuming he has a team with him here as well, so we need to make sure we bring in the cavalry."

*****

Trent wore a hoodie. His beard was tucked into the neck of the sweater; he looked like he had just finished a workout. He stood above Pierce and Kelly, leaning on the balcony railing. He pulled the directional microphone out of his phone jack and slipped it back into his sweatshirt pocket.

Just a few taps on the screen sent the audio recording to his boss, and followed up with a text, 'Pierce male, Kelly female, agency unknown.'

They have no idea who they are dealing with. If he had known it was his last day on Earth, he would have finished that drink.

CHAPTER 20

PRAGUE, CZECH REPUBLIC

In chess, an amateur can think about three moves ahead. A master can think about seven moves ahead, anticipating the moves of their opponent simultaneously.

A grandmaster thinks eleven to fifteen moves ahead.

Aphid stood at the large window in his decadent office overlooking his hidden facility below. He had spared no expense constructing this building inside of the warehouse. The dark wood paneling met with ornate Persian rugs laid on a hardwood floor. The odor of pipe tobacco reminded him of his childhood home, and he cherished the little time he got to spend in this office alone.

He gently pulled the teabag out of his steaming glass mug and dropped it into a wastebasket at his side. He peered down into the facility he had created inside of the warehouse. He genuinely cared about these people. Dead or alive, they made a sacrifice to improve the world, and records would show, in the end, that no matter how many people Aphid killed, he served to bring about the new awakening of the people of the world. He didn't care for notoriety, only truth. Sometimes, to show the full extent of the truth, extreme measures had to be taken. Larger plans like this required intellect and strategic prowess that very few possessed.

> *I'm a lone grandmaster in a sea of morons; the only salvation these people have with the courage to change the world.*

This was how Aphid saw the world. There was an ample supply of amateurs–those who preferred, subconsciously, to let others do most of the thinking for them. This was especially true in America, where mind control was rampant. The tools they used to control the public were so seemingly beneficial that people willingly submitted their data—and the keys to their minds—along with it.

Aphid had been a keen observer of humans. As he grew older, it became more apparent that the number of real-life grandmasters was dwindling. As he aged, he saw less and less of the men who once made up the honest-living and clean-thinking society. It was depressing, but it made his particular skills more powerful as the controllable masses increased in number.

The Americans had created him, and he saw it as his duty to show them who they were—filthy. With American politics having become nothing more than a reality show—a group of people solely interested in their own power and status. The American media injected fearful imaginings into people's minds like a drug. The fear and hatred made them focus on their *own* lives, creating apathy toward the forces hell-bent on possessing their souls. This maniacal drive America had to control its citizens had become another part of everyday life.

People just accepted it—traded their security for convenience, their freedom for comfort.

People had turned so far into themselves that they became offended at things that had no basis in the real world. They were becoming fat, fearful, compliant, and stupid. How easy it would be to overcome them all with a problem that couldn't be solved by a petition on social media.

Regardless of how much trouble the politicians were in, inevitably, a mass shooting would happen, the focus of the nation would shift, and the indiscretions of the elite would fade into the never-ending barrage of news. The severe and far-reaching nature of the conduct of the American government was no match for the child-like attention span of the American people.

Their inflated sense of self-worth unlocked their true potential for manipulation by their government. This awakening would change the future and expose this government for what they had done. A loud knock rang out at his door.

"Come in," Aphid said.

An older, frail-looking man entered the office wearing a wrinkled, white lab coat. He removed his reading glasses and let them hang from the lanyard around his neck.

"We've made final changes. The lights flashing at the beginning of the video were brought down to 29 times a second and we increased the success rate by 12%."

"Thank you, Bazil. How long is the video?"

"We've tailored the video to reflect the research documents from the Americans, sir. It's seventy-four seconds, starts in black and white, and has quick-scrolling text on the screen."

"You've changed history, Bazil. I couldn't be prouder. Your mother would be beaming with pride."

The old man closed his eyes and thanked Aphid for the kind words.

Aphid knew what the man needed to hear. As a true friend, Aphid knew he wouldn't have to kill the man after the operation to keep information from leaking. The rest of the team would be fine to continue; they had been given so much misinformation and counterintelligence. Any investigation would turn into a goose chase to every corner of the earth.

When Aphid had interviewed one of the girls he referred to as specimens earlier in the month—before live testing began—he became quite fond of her. Her youth brought new life to him. She had long blonde hair and flawless California skin. He enjoyed her physically and emotionally. She acted as though the toll of her captivity was dampened by the care he provided her. On the evening he allowed her to sleep in his fortified corner of the warehouse, however, she took his kindness for weakness, and tried to stab him with a silver letter opener that had been in his family since the 1700s.

He would never forget her face when she attacked him. She ran naked from the bathroom with fear and rage in her eyes. He admired her spirit. His first instinct was to let her attack and then simply kill her, but he decided to see how fast the phrase from HIG would work.

Without spilling a drop of his wine, he shouted the phrase and watched her young, dimpled expression go from rage to confusion to complete and utter relaxation. She stood there at his bedside, naked and waiting for a command, the silver letter opener dropping to the floor.

She needed to be taught a lesson, so he took her to dinner at Hotel Carlo IV in Prague. There, as she prepared to walk off the roof, he saw that somewhere in the recesses of her mind, something fought the action–something resisted. But she complied.

He turned to Bazil, who stood in the doorway, allowing his long-time friend the opportunity to let his mind wander.

"Bazil, bring the final group of specimens in as soon as the rooms are clean and have the staff prepare whatever meal they desire."

"Of course, sir. I've had the men pack your bags as you asked. Are there any other things you'd like?"

"Thank you. Yes. The silver letter opener on the nightstand. Pack it in my briefcase. And the picture above the desk here. This needs to be brought to Iceland when we leave."

The old man turned to the large picture hanging on the wall behind the chair at his desk. It was the size of a normal poster, but horizontal. It was solid black except for one hazy figure of a man in the center. The figure was a nondescript silhouette of a man in a suit and tie. The color of the man reminded Aphid of television static. The figure's face was blacked out. The only clear things about the photo were large, bold numbers written across the man's chest in black. '1572.'

"The CIA released this photo to the public in 1972. They spent a lifetime trying to determine its origin before they eventually determined the public could view it," Aphid said.

Bazil eyed the photo for a moment. "It looks like a nightmare. They only released this picture?"

"Two pictures, actually. They were mostly identical, apart from the numbers on their chests. One of them read '1569' and the other read '1572.' They made them public to the intelligence community first, hoping someone would figure out the significance of the dates, and what they had to do with the collapse of the Soviet Union. No one ever came forward or discovered their meaning. The CIA then made them public in hopes that it would stir discussion, and someone would eventually figure out the mystery and let them in on the secret they could never figure out."

"Is there a hidden code in the image or something?"

Bazil leaned in and pulled his reading glasses onto his face, eyeing the strange, fuzzy pattern of the ghostly man in the photo. Bazil's olive Egyptian skin had begun to give way to time. At 65, his long face hung atop a thin frame. His hair and beard hadn't seen attention in some time.

"No hidden code. The KGB found this image on an agent who had been captured in the Soviet Union. An American. The two images were the front and back cover of a pocket-sized manual. The man who'd possessed it had somehow removed the inner contents of the book before his capture."

"Like a spy book?"

"Yes, Bazil."

"I bet he ate it—digested it with stomach acid somehow. Maybe into a toilet."

"Very possible. It's still classified, but *we* have the records. There *is* a part of the story that truly resembles a nightmare. The two Soviet agents holding the man captive inexplicably committed suicide, simultaneously. The man disappeared. The CIA recovered the book covers during a raid of the prison."

Bazil adjusted his glasses and lowered his eyebrows. "So, it's like what we are doing here?" he asked.

"Very much like what we are doing here, on an extreme level."

Aphid sipped his tea and sat down in the sitting area, motioning for Bazil to sit. He eyed the progress below through the large glass window and again said a silent prayer for the young people who were about to help him change the world.

"My friend, we are fighting an enemy that dates to the 1500s. This book we are speaking about was a reference manual for covert operatives. They work *above* the government and consider themselves higher in integrity than could ever be voted upon, decided, or debated amongst the public. False gods.

"They can talk you into doing anything. *Anything,* Bazil. Things that make our research look like a game of backgammon amongst children. Their operatives have swung elections, controlled the movement of nuclear power, and even decided which country receives chemical weapons, all by speaking to one person for only a moment."

Bazil shook his head. "The 1500s. How big is this group? How can they make an impact like this without government support? We *can* stop them, Aphid."

"Our project *is* going to stop them. It will expose them and their families—their children. Those two photographs," Aphid said, "are a reference to the beginnings and what could have been the end of this secretive group of people. They call themselves HIG. No one knows what that stands for—but I do."

Bazil stared, hoping Aphid would continue. Aphid took another sip of tea and crossed his legs. He gently pulled a cigarette out of a gold box on the table in front of him, and Bazil scrambled to light it for him.

"The numbers on those men are *years* representing the two anonymous men who began the HIG in 1569. In that first year, a man named Roberto Ridolfi, a banker, became involved in the planning of a major rebellion in England. His plot was to influence and persuade a small group of people to kill Queen Elizabeth, and get Mary, the Queen of Scots, to marry Thomas Howard, a man who later became enthralled with the ability to persuade government groups.

"Thomas Howard was the 4th Duke of Norfolk. He and Ridolfi built a group of men who turned the persuasion of government officials into a science. They kept their research hidden and built a small, secret organization around the teachings. When Thomas Howard's plot was discovered, he was captured, tortured, and eventually beheaded in the second numbered year, 1572, you'll see in the other photo. It was this four-year endeavor that formed what is now a large-scale operation. This was the cover of the HIG training manual. The Ridolfi plot is how it all began."

Bazil sat in complete silence.

"These people hide in the shadows like cowards. I have two of them about to be captured in California now, and we'll have answers. In the meantime, I'm stepping up operational speed, and we will launch the video before sunrise in California. I've sent a man to

Yorktown, Virginia as well to cut off the head of the snake."

CHAPTER 21
SAN JOSE, CALIFORNIA

The Central Police Station came into view on Mission Street, and Pierce pulled the SUV into the main parking lot.

In the front office, two lone officers sat behind a thick glass barrier and welcomed them courteously. Two vagrants sat against the opposite wall. One of them held a plastic bag full of partially smoked cigarettes, the other held a rolled blanket with a sleeping cat's head protruding from the center.

Kelly approached the window, but Pierce slapped her butt in a way that made her stop talking. As she turned and looked at Pierce with a surprised smile, he ignored her and leaned into the hole in the window. Kelly recognized the words coming out of his mouth immediately.

Phrase Twelve.

He spoke the words while slapping the glass simultaneously to ensure their subconscious recognized this as an unusual event, thereby absorbing what he was saying on a much deeper level. Kelly had been trained to resist the phrase but found herself struggling to pull herself back to reality for a moment. She pulled her lower lip into her mouth and bit down until she couldn't take it.

Pierce continued talking as he pulled Kelly back into reality by her arm. She lurched forward and heard him speaking to the officers behind the bulletproof glass as if they were his children.

"...and that's fine, John. You and Aaron can do that. I'm happy you're glad to give that to me and it's completely fine...there's always that feeling that you're able to recognize now that we tend to *get completely confused* remembering...this with me...here is something like that, and I know you both work very hard, and I'm so thankful for your *service...to me*...that's something amazing, what you guys...do...so much for me...*go above and beyond* the call. Thank you. Thank you both. John, Aaron, you're amazing, thank you, guys. I hope you have a great day."

Kelly watched as Pierce took a small stack of papers from an officer and mimicked a fist-bump through the bulletproof glass.

"...and you guys were helping so many people, and these two are here and you guys are great."

The bewildered officer shifted his focus from Pierce to the two grungy guys sitting in their lobby and began calling them up. One of them, the guy with the cigarettes, stared at Kelly in a way that felt like sexual assault. He smiled as they left. Kelly imagined making him eat the cigarettes he'd collected.

Pierce, obviously on a mission, said nothing but "passenger" and motioned to the passenger side of the SUV. Kelly climbed back into the vehicle with a newfound sense of purpose, and Pierce pulled the vehicle back onto Mission Street.

"I had you ride shotgun because I know you can piece all of this stuff together a lot faster than I can."

"Pierce, I—"

"I need you to look through those documents. Find me a destination and a man to kill. I'll drive toward downtown until that happens."

Kelly sighed and kicked her dress shoes off into the floorboard, tucking her legs under her. Pierce pulled the car back into the street and flicked on the headlights.

Kelly poured through the stack of police reports, speed-reading the contents, images, and data they contained on the missing-persons reports.

"What's your most embarrassing memory, Pierce?" she asked, continuing to leaf through the papers.

She knew her efforts to get Pierce into a more relaxed mood were transparent. He would probably also know she asked him about a childhood memory to pull him away from his feelings of guilt.

"I got caught cheating on an algebra exam—sophomore year," Pierce said.

"You cheated?" Kelly swung her head toward Pierce.

Pierce shot a glance back over the center console. "It was an honest answer to your silly question. What was yours?"

Kelly searched his expression for sincerity and decided to be honest. "I farted accidentally on a date a month ago."

Pierce smiled and glanced at her to make sure she was serious. "Jesus."

"Yeah. He pretended not to hear it, but people two tables away heard it. I excused myself to the ladies' room and left through the back door of the restaurant. Haven't seen him since. I was mortified."

Pierce let out a short laugh and turned onto a narrow street toward the freeway.

"He knew you were a human going into the date. The jig was already up. If he's the guy that thinks girls don't fart, it's an extreme red flag and you know that."

"True. But it's still the most embarrassed I've ever been. On another note, I'm seeing *our* guy's name here. The local police tracked him to a local Holiday Inn. He's got a military record that is redacted like a Senate Intelligence report."

"Name?"

"Trent Cavender."

"We can track him if we–"

The entire vehicle floated forward in mid-air before a massive, skeleton-shaking force jerked them into exploding airbags. The burn of the airbag ripped into her face like a sunburn; her eyes filled with tears. The back tires of the vehicle came back down to the earth with a force that slammed Kelly back into her seat. Her vision was so blurred she couldn't see Pierce, but she could tell he was moving.

A large recycling truck had pulled in front of them, and in the headlights, the door of the truck opened. A person jumped out and began closing the distance to her window with a handgun drawn. She wrestled with the seat belt to draw her weapon as deafening gunshots shattered the windshield.

She didn't feel anything, and her Five-seveN pistol was in her hand. Pierce fired through the windshield into the man's face, and his voice boomed into the ringing silence between them.

"Unbuckle your seatbelt, wipe your eyes, get out, and stay low. Take that man's weapon, and if he's still breathing, use Phrase One as loud as you can."

Kelly sprang out of the vehicle and wiped away the rush of tears from the impact of the airbag. Her bare feet met the crumbles of glass in the street, it somehow made her more focused than ever before. The man on the ground was burly, clean-shaven, and wearing high-end body armor.

He was still breathing. A small bullet hole in his left cheek had paralyzed most of his body, and his left pupil was dilated to the edges of his eye. Blood trickled down his face to the pavement below.

Kelly was astonished at how automatic her training had become. She vividly remembered what her instructors at HIG had taught her: "Two chest–two head." They called it the hearts and minds campaign. *Stop the heart. Stop the mind.*

Kelly had been trained to use Phrase One in extreme situations. She had seen videos of what it could do. Coma was a definite possibility; they had called it the 'Esdaile State.' The only issue was that it took roughly nine seconds to speak the entire phrase.

She rolled the large man to one side and pulled his wallet from his pocket. Phrase One *required* knowledge of the person's name, and a few other things like the person's preferred vocabulary. Nathan was the name on the license.

Kelly sized him up, determining the primary psychosocial needs of the man, she profiled his deepest fears, and what words to use. His shirt was one size too small, and the man's muscles were visible through the fabric.

He likes to feel powerful. Fears feeling small and being made to look weak.

The man's watch was set five minutes ahead of Kelly's, which was always accurate. His fingernails were manicured, and he had recently gotten a haircut.

Concerned with personal appearance and interested in self-development. Probably fears judgment and being seen by others as lazy or careless.

The words left her mouth at the highest volume she had ever used.

Two words into the phrase, another gunshot exploded into the air. Kelly continued, hoping that if Pierce didn't survive, the passenger of the truck would be affected by the rest of the phrase. She persisted with a determination and calm that surprised her.

She watched this man–Nathan. His one working eye rolled back into his head. He started to hum like he had lost control of neurological function. She wanted to look away. She just wanted to kill him.

Whoever sent this team had no idea what Pierce and Kelly were capable of. But now they needed information. Kelly peered under the chassis of the truck. Pierce had killed the man on the other side of it, so Kelly needed this man alive. The phrase had imprinted her voice into his brain like a duckling imprints on its mother.

She rocked her feet back onto the bits of glass in the street. The man in front of her was about to give her information to put an end to what could become a huge fucking disaster.

Kelly slid her pistol back into its holster and knelt beside him.

His chest stopped moving. Then, a heaving inhale that sounded like death–like a person trying to breathe through a plastic bag.

Agonal respirations. He's almost dead.

She pulled her skirt up and straddled the gasping man's body and began a series of chest compressions that rivaled any workout she had ever done. She didn't have long, and used his name again to ask him who he worked for.

Pierce came around the truck with a duffel bag and stack of papers he had discovered.

Again, the terrifying sounds of agonal breathing began, the body's last-ditch effort to save itself by using the nervous system to force breathing.

Kelly stood and pulled a sanitizing wipe from her bra, ripped open the packet and cleaned her hands.

"Leave him. We've got a lot here to go through," Pierce said, holding up the duffel bag.

*****

Two hundred yards away, Trent sat on his motorcycle, recalculating who he was dealing with. Aphid hadn't told him to expect operators—people who had this level of skill. He watched the skinny girl and the man approach a civilian's vehicle that had stopped to check on the accident. The man approached the window of the vehicle, holding up some sort of identification, and the driver of the car motioned for them to get in. They loaded bags from the wrecked Ford Explorer and climbed into the rear seat of the good Samaritan's car.

Trent started the bike's engine and drove.

These weren't normal people.

Plans need to change. Now.

CHAPTER 22

YORKTOWN, VIRGINIA

The sun was setting in Yorktown. Alex had been up for almost two days trying to keep the team informed and dispatching every available operative to San Jose. His office and his living quarters were luckily in the same building at HIG, but he had no time to sleep.

If Phrase Seven was used on a mass scale, it had the potential to not only expose HIG for the first time but could end up as the most extensive loss of life in history.

Deidra was in over her head and had been equally busy running through her intelligence contacts overseas. She had never used extreme HIG persuasion phrasing on foreign nationals over the phone to get information, but she was hell-bent on ensuring she brought whomever it was to justice.

In less than a day, she managed to track the digital files, and even several funding channels, to a small area in Prague called 'Prague Nine.' She burst into Alex's office and gave him the update.

"I'm going to head to Prague with Jennifer. She's fluent in Czech. We have a small security team there in the city."

"Deidra, I don't think you should be going anywhere. We need you here. You're the Director. I know it's—"

Deidra held up a finger. "I'm going. This isn't something we can sit on. I don't know what is happening there in Prague, but all the data and funding sources are leading to the same fucking neighborhood."

Alex sighed, defeated. "I'll keep things together here."

Deidra nodded, composed considering everything she was juggling. "Thanks for this, Alex. I'm not sure I'd have survived this without your help. I'll have the plane ready in an hour." She hesitated. "Thank you for everything, actually. I've learned to be a stronger woman because of you, and you've given me almost every personal growth spurt I've had."

Alex nodded. "Deidra, I'm proud of you, and you could have handled this all on your own without a single bit of help. Please stay safe out there."

"Thanks, Alex. I will. I'll keep you posted. I'm going dark on all communications till we are in the air." She folded a raincoat over her arm, turned, and walked into the hallway. Her slim frame and muscular features hadn't ever changed. Although she was a grandmother now, it certainly didn't look like it. The sleepless work of Director hadn't begun to show yet. Alex hoped it never would.

A few heartbeats later, her car started outside under the lit carport near the kitchen door. The ominous sound of the Suburban's tires on gravel faded. He stood, wondering how quickly he could go to sleep. The teams were beginning to converge on San Jose, and that with unlimited access to police, they would quickly narrow the search within an hour of their arrival in the city. Meanwhile, Pierce and Kelly had to stay alive and get him answers so he could direct the teams for a strike operation.

It wasn't a minute before the light inside of a glass brick on his desk turned from green to red, indicating Deidra had driven through the driveway exit.

A beep from the hallway penetrated the silence. A door had been opened near the kitchen.

Alex leaned forward and pulled a pristine H&K USP 45 from the large rectangular magnet under his desk and flipped off the weapon's safety.

Without a sound, he stepped into the hallway and approached the door that alarmed, the same door Deidra used to exit. It looked secure; Alex continued his advance.

At about ten feet from the door, everything appeared to be undisturbed. Alex's heart rate climbed as he neared the doorway, aware that around eighty percent of killings happened in doorways. This one, in particular, left no escape as the hallway provided little room to maneuver left or right to avoid gunfire from an assailant outside in the drive.

Alex braced himself, readying the heavy handgun for action. When he came to within about two feet of the doorway, he looked through the windows, and it was a few seconds into his search before he noticed something that ignited a sense of terror he hadn't felt in decades.

The door was shut, but a strip of duct tape protruded from the frame of the door latch mechanism.

Someone had placed a strip of tape there while Deidra exited the compound, preventing the door from locking itself.

A sound from behind jolted his whole body. A strong metallic taste bloomed in his mouth as he spun around, preparing to level his weapon.

His hand gripping the gun no longer obeyed his commands. His breathing became labored and difficult. Attempting to lift his arm did no good, his uncooperative limbs occupied his focus until a figure moved in front of him down the hall. He leaned against the wall for support and slid down until he could rest on the floor. He had to sit.

The figure in front of him casually checked his wristwatch and began taking slow, unhurried steps toward him.

Alex's chin was wet. As he took in another breath, he realized he had been shot. His life was spraying out of the exit wound in his chest as he tried to inhale. He hadn't felt the bullet. The man in front of him continued closing in, holding a neoprene-wrapped, silenced pistol.

A dark mask obscured the attacker's face. He wore large, over-the-ear hearing protection, and didn't speak a word.

Alex tried desperately to haul the leaden gun into action. He managed to pull his finger hard enough to fire a round into the hallway wall. He knew it might alert a few of the personnel working below, but with the soundproofing in the gargantuan house, he wasn't hopeful.

As a cloud of powder from the erupting drywall settled into a quiet blanket of dust on his legs, he took in one final, agonizing breath as he watched the man level the pistol.

Alex closed his eyes.

CHAPTER 23
SAN JOSE, CALIFORNIA

Trent had seen a lot of operators in his time, but these people were different. This little pixie-looking girl had done *something* to that man. They used a trick like the hypnosis stuff he took from Aphid's video.

He'd pulled the Triumph motorcycle into a parking garage and ridden it to the roof. Trent pulled out his phone and dialed a number to reach Aphid directly. This needed to be stopped.

The number rang into a switching station in India in a secure building. The cellular call was then routed through an audio system that ran through an internet channel layered far into the dark web. It was a secure line that looked as though a call was coming from a number in Vancouver, Canada. The audio was scrambled so that any listener could only hear a high-pitched sound unless they had a phone decrypting the signal. It made everyone sound like a mechanical robot over a call, but it was what Aphid deemed as the most secure way to communicate.

"Yes?"

Aphid's voice was unrecognizable over this system, so Trent had to memorize a special number. Seventeen was the number they had arranged for the call. Whatever number Trent mentioned over the phone, Aphid would respond with another number that would equal seventeen if the two were added together.

Trent spoke first. "Nine."

Aphid immediately responded, "Eight."

"Sir, we have a problem. Two people, maybe more, are somehow tracking the operation. They took out your team about fifty minutes ago. Local time is 8 PM here. I'm not due to complete phase five until tomorrow, and I don't know how many operators they have on this."

There was a pause before Aphid spoke.

"Describe the operators who stopped our team," the robotic voice countered.

"Sir, it was the same two from the hotel. Pierce and Kelly were the names they used. The male was about forty, five-foot-nine. The female was like five-three, shorter hair, maybe a hundred-ten pounds. Both of them have been trained well. I could have probably killed one of them, but I wouldn't have made it through both."

"Did you see anything unusual?"

"Like what?"

"Like something you haven't seen before. Something you may not have expected?"

Aphid was prodding to see if they had used that hypnosis shit. Trent thought carefully before he answered.

"Sir, the only thing I saw out of the ordinary was that the woman did something to the larger man on our team. She used drugs or something. Our operative seemed to be in some kind of..."

"Trance?" Aphid prompted encouragingly.

"Yes, sir. Like a zombie or something."

"You did well to keep your distance. You're critical to this operation. And you wouldn't have killed any of them. You would have shot *yourself* in the head if you even got near them. Don't fucking approach them. Ever. I'll send a special team in to get them taken care of."

"Yes, sir."

Aphid paused again before Trent heard the robotic voice crackle once more. "I need you to finish this. We need to change the timeline. You will have a new target package in five minutes. I need it done immediately. It is the final phase. The money will transfer immediately upon completion. I'll see you back at home. Keep me posted. You're my asset. Don't fucking approach them. Don't get within five hundred meters of them. Do you understand?"

"I understand."

Trent could probably take them out if he wanted. He'd been in special operations units for a long time, and he'd seen every level of operator. These people were like any other, and he knew they bled when shot, like anyone else. But he'd listen to the old man. Something told him it was the safest bet.

A tone indicated the call was terminated.

Half an hour later, Trent pulled his motorcycle into the parking lot of the West Valley Fair shopping mall, where he had parked a minivan. Minivans had turned out to be an indispensable resource. They were unassuming, held a massive amount of gear, and they were surprisingly agile if you got a good one.

He chose a gray minivan and loaded it with everything he might need for an assignment. The rear contained duffle bags for different operations and a long, waterproof container that housed his prized Barnett Vengeance Crossbow. Not the most ideal weapon in a gunfight, but it was quieter than a whisper and could deliver death at up to a hundred yards without a sound.

With security cameras at malls, he had to keep his scarf close to his face, and he couldn't park next to the minivan and get into it. Even a dipshit security guard would see that as suspicious. He parked the bike one row over, pretended to check his phone for about five minutes, and kept an eye on every vehicle nearby to ensure no surveillance was being done on the van. Once satisfied, he walked into a BestBuy and went to the bathroom. He put his motorcycle helmet in the trash, flipped his dark green reversible jacket inside out, making it orange, and walked back outside to the van.

He started the van and immediately prepared to evade any surveillance teams, but there were none.

Idiots.

Trent couldn't figure out why Aphid feared these people so much. He exited the mall parking lot and pulled into traffic. He found a parking area in front of a nearby hotel and pulled in.

His phone showed two new messages. He opened the first message and downloaded a high-resolution image of a golden crown.

Nice.

He opened the decrypting app and pulled the image into it. A seventeen-page document opened. A new target. A photo of a man, and the target package detailed known properties, friends, family, location of children's schools, and even maps of the homes the man lived in around California.

Trent read the name, and a cold sweat enveloped his body.

This man was the CEO of Follow-Me, the largest social media company in America. David Morris. He was on television daily and had homes in almost every major city. That wasn't what scared him, however. The man had a security team that consisted of kind, courteous, patient, intelligent killers. All of them looked normal, but Trent had friends who had left the military and entered this business. They were real-life killers. He knew he'd have to take a few of these guys out, but he was more worried about what the target package commanded him to do.

This led him to a second file. It wasn't a high-resolution image. It was a raw video file protected by a password. The password to unlock the video, the document said, was his target's social security number followed by the man's bank account number, with no spaces. Trent knew this might be the only man that could unlock the video.

His task was simple. Just get the guy to open this file and put his target on speakerphone with Aphid.

Aphid would take over, then Trent could kill the social media CEO, and head back to Prague with a fresh bank account that would allow him to do whatever he pleased for the next twenty years.

Trent looked up the man's address. It was twenty-nine minutes away.

He shifted the minivan back into gear and pulled back into the streets. This place disgusted Trent. False displays of open arms and welcoming hearts, while homeless villages flourished next to wealthy areas, trash blew in the streets, and the divide between wealthy and poor rivaled that of India.

America *did* need a wakeup call.

*****

Pierce released the driver they had persuaded to take them to the hotel. The woman was pleasant and thanked them for the trip and the conversation, which she would later recall very little of.

He and Kelly managed to acquire a new vehicle and drove until they pulled into the driveway of one of Pierce's closest friends—a man named Eric. He served with Pierce in the CIA fifteen years ago, but it felt like a lifetime since then. Eric had amassed a following while conducting international negotiations in Dubai and decided to leave the service when a Saudi company made him an offer to run their operations in California.

His house wasn't only secure, it was empty. Eric kept the house, but lived in San Diego full time. He had given Pierce the door passcode and sent him a document that had everything he would need to know to stay in the house, apparently something he had put together for friends and family.

The door buzzed open and the two made their way inside. Pierce surveyed the floor-to-ceiling glass walls and expansive, pristine interior. It looked like something out of a movie. This gigantic house was something he could never picture himself living in.

He and Kelly made their way into the kitchen and sat on calfskin barstools. Pierce slid his laptop onto the stone counter, flipping it open.

Kelly slid back in her seat and pulled off her shoes.

"I'm never taking my shoes off in the car again. They didn't tell me that in training."

Pierce eyed her feet. "You okay?"

Kelly pulled a small chunk of glass from her heel. "From the street."

"Jesus. Let me look."

Kelly propped her feet on the counter in front of Pierce. They were covered in little scrapes. He flicked on the flashlight of his phone and leaned in close. He extracted a small sliver of glass from the outer edge of her little toe.

"There's no more glass, thank God. Those windows are designed to break into crumbles." Pierce said.

Pierce retrieved an antiseptic spray from his bag and sprayed it on her feet.

"Get some socks on and change into your boots."

She fixated on Pierce. For the first time, he saw fear in her green eyes.

"They're sending teams, right?"

"Yes. Deidra's sending everyone. They should be here before sunrise."

Kelly glanced back at her feet on the counter. She scrunched her red, painted toes.

"I'm going to need a pedicure after this shit."

"We'll put it on the HIG credit card," Pierce said with a wink.

Kelly spun around to go collect their bags from the car.

Pierce had no trouble finding the coffee and shoved a pod into the machine. It began brewing as his phone vibrated in his pocket.

It was a full text message.

Alex killed. HIG detained killer. Details obtained. Call in.

Time stopped. His heart hammered at his ribcage with every beat. He stood motionless in the kitchen and forced himself to get control of his breathing.

He gently set the phone down, turned toward the freezer, pulled it open, and found a fresh, frosted bottle of vodka.

He let out a long sigh as he watched the liquid pour out into the glass. He tapped the screen on his phone until it began to ring. Mariel

Thomas, a senior agent at HIG, answered the phone.

“Pierce?” Mariel’s voice was soft and empathetic.

“Hey.”

“He’s dead, Pierce. They fucking shot him in the back.” Mariel’s voice trembled; he knew she was trying to hold it together. “I know he was like a father to you.”

His lips tightened, trying to keep himself centered. He squeezed his eyes shut to hold it all back and leaned against the counter.

After several long seconds, Mariel whispered into the phone, “Pierce?”

Pierce took in a full breath and composed himself. “He’ll be missed. This won’t go unpunished. What can we do here?”

He took the first sip of ice-cold vodka. The burn that trickled down his throat felt like an old friend.

“Pierce, one of the guys downstairs heard a shot and hit the button.”

The ‘button’ was an actual button at HIG that activated a neutralization system in the house. If pressed, a mixture of gasses mostly comprised of airborne fentanyl and the anesthetic halothane were ejected from every doorway and continued to fill the house. The staff drew gas masks and were to either search the house or remain in place, based on their level of training.

"We got him, Pierce. He provided a lot of information, but we need to get this to you immediately."

"Will you keep him alive until I get back?"

"I can't do that. We don't do that. I *can* tell you he won't even know how to speak when we're finished. I'm going to completely wipe him."

"What information did he give us?" Pierce wiped his cheeks.

"We traced everything back to Prague. Deidra is on her way with Jennifer to sort it out. Jennifer speaks fluent Czech. The key findings led to a single list that was purchased on the dark web. The list appeared to be totally harmless until we saw a name on it. David Morris."

"The social media guy?"

"Yes. We found his home address and all kinds of personal info on him. We know San Jose is the hotbed right now, and from that entire list, that man is the only one within a few hours' reach. Even more, the group who sold the list was in an apartment building in Mexico City, and the entire building caught fire about six hours ago. They're all dead."

"So, he's some kind of target?"

"We think the phrase that was taken from your iPad has been weaponized somehow. This could be an attempt to test it on him for public impact, or some other kind of political message."

Kelly walked into the kitchen. She had changed into operational clothing. Her brunette hair was swept back into a short ponytail, her body armor cinched tight across her body. She studied him with concern and set the bags down before she joined him at the bar.

Mariel continued. "I need you to get to him. We've sent out a message through the FBI to all the local social media companies' senior personnel to stay secure tonight. I don't know how the FBI handles this stuff, but I'm guessing that they won't broadcast it on national television. They will keep it quiet. It might take hours to get to the CEOs, if it gets to them at all."

"We can get to him tonight. It's about 9:00 PM here. We can be at his address in..."

Pierce tapped on his phone, pulling up the data from Mariel.

"...looks like about forty minutes."

"Pierce. There's another thing we got from the guy during the interrogation here."

"What's that?"

"He told us the man he works for is in Prague—in his seventies. Has an American accent. Goes by the name Aphid."

"Is it Timothy Briggs?"

"We aren't sure, but it's possible."

"Okay. Thanks. Keep me posted. Kelly and I are heading out now."

"The teams from HIG will be there soon. You can direct them through me, or I can send them to the house you're in now."

"Thanks, Mariel. I'll let you know what we find. For now, have the teams on standby."

Pierce ended the call. Kelly looked at him expectantly. He grabbed the glass of vodka and poured it into the sink. His breathing shuddered.

"Who's Timothy Briggs?" Kelly asked

"He funded a few terror operations and went off the radar a year ago. We think he's in Prague. Canadian. He commands a little army of elite, retired military guys. He's a fucking nightmare and we don't know a ton about him other than what I just told you."

Kelly shook her head and eyed Pierce. "That's not what we need right now. If you get dressed, you can fill me in on the way to this social media guy's house."

Pierce's phone buzzed.

It was a message from Alex Frost.

CHAPTER 24
PRAGUE, CZECH REPUBLIC

The cabin of the plane was a prison to Deidra. Despite its spacious cabin and decor, she needed out. She needed air. The plush, gray carpet, the leather couches, and the coffee table she had custom-built for the plane all mocked her.

She received the news about Alex about two hours before the plane touched down in Prague. Despite her attempts to contain herself, she had lost all control. Jennifer Goram, her close friend, and Senior Agent at HIG, had kept her from forcing the plane back to Virginia. Deidra had lain on the floor of the plane and sobbed the final few hours of their flight.

As the plane taxied into the large Euro Jet hangar, Deidra turned to Jennifer. "Don't say a word about this flight, please."

The two HIG pilots opened the plane's door. Jennifer pulled a coat over her thin but muscular frame and the wind outside the plane blew her blonde hair to one side. Their local security team transported them the ten kilometers to a safehouse HIG maintained in Prague.

Deidra knew this was the only way to finish it all. Whether it was Pierce's iPad or some other way, they would have stolen the information somehow. Still, Pierce would blame himself.

As they shuffled up the short walkway to the small house on Choceňská, she said a silent prayer that she could finish this before things got out of control. The HIG safehouse was falling apart. Decaying stone walls, overgrown grass, and dirty windows made the home look almost abandoned. Deidra picked this location not only because of its distance from the center of Prague, but because it was also less than a hundred yards from a water tower that housed a stunning array of government and intelligence antennas.

The team at HIG could hook in through an eight-foot antenna on the roof of the safehouse and monitor operations on the ground.

Deidra and Jennifer only needed to bring a locked black case into the house, screw in a wire that looked like a cable TV hookup, and plug the box into the wall. It would run until someone unplugged it, and it couldn't be traced because it was so close to the signal pollution from the water tower's antennas.

If things went south, the impact would be global. The news would pick it up first, and social media would do what it did best—capitalize on fear, spread mistrust, and raise advertising prices for ads appearing alongside horrific stories.

"You okay?" Jennifer placed a hand on Deidra's shoulder.

"I'm fine. I'm prepared to do whatever needs to be done here to prevent this from devolving even further. If someone weaponized this thing, the loss of life alone could be in the tens of millions."

"I know," Jennifer said as she typed a code into the keypad on the house's door. "I just want you to know I'm here if you need anything."

"Ma'am?" The lead security man stood several feet behind them. "I'm going to have the men here until you're ready to go. We have six men on the house and two near the front gate for overwatch. Dylan will bring your case in."

"Thanks, Mike. Shouldn't be long."

It was a two-bedroom house that HIG had used as a command center to stop civil unrest in Prague earlier in the previous year. Tens of thousands of citizens flooded the streets. What the public didn't know was that the protest was preventing the transport of a terror suspect being held in the basement of a municipal building southwest of the city.

Cheap furniture decorated the house. It looked like it had been acquired from a hospital waiting room. Two steel beds, and laminate floors gave way to nauseating green walls. One of the security men brought in the large black container.

After a quick shower, Deidra rejoined Jennifer in the living room, where Jennifer had set up two laptops. A cable ran to an antenna she'd attached to the window with a suction cup.

Jennifer looked up at Deidra, concerned. "You sure you're up for this trip?"

"Let's find wherever this is based out of and level the fucking building. You speak the language here; I'll need you at your best. If you need to sleep, or you need anything..."

Jennifer smiled. Deidra was back in the game. In reality, it wasn't the catastrophe motivating her to move forward with such force, it was a burning desire she would never admit to anyone: witnessing the destruction of the people who had killed her friend and mentor.

Jennifer flipped open one of the laptops and booted up a program running on an external hard drive. After almost a minute of static, a window of a video chat program opened. A man in a suit was positioned in front of a bookcase with a small lamp illuminating the desk in front of him.

"I hope the flight was good."

Steven Gibbs was the senior intelligence officer at HIG. His contacts in the CIA were still like family, and his access was uninhibited. He managed to serve his time without a single partisan comment, and never became involved in such discussions. Anyone at HIG knew both sides were full of shit.

"Flight was great, Steven. Any news?"

"Yes, ma'am." He pulled out a manila folder. "Three sources confirmed that there is about a three-block radius we're working with. Our file had a call-home feature enabled, but we never received a call since it was stolen. For the first time in months, the Phrase Seven file was connected to a computer that is on a network. They must have been using standalone machines until now."

"Brilliant. Can we get an address? We're just northwest of the city in a small green area. Jennifer and I can be there in fifteen."

"No address yet. Prague is a modern city, but the electricity and networks in this part are still run like Thailand. Everyone steals electricity, and the electrical poles are a jumbled mess of homemade electrical wires and cables. We are working on it now. We'll keep you posted."

"Great. Thanks, Steven."

"I'm looking into the data we passed to Pierce and Kelly. They are running down the best lead we have. We are pretty certain David Morris is a prime target. They might do something to him on camera. I don't know. We sent an anonymous message for him to bump up security and get out of town if possible. No response."

"In terms of our operation here, what area of Prague are we talking about, Steven?"

"It's a place called 'Prague Nine,' a few miles northeast of Prague proper. There's a lot of abandoned industrial buildings. I'd like to get a drone up in the air there. The security team has a signals scanner, and I can put someone who actually knows what all that is on the call with you."

"Great. We both slept a bit on the plane. We will get situated. Get those computer boys ready to go."

"Thanks, Deidra. There's a hotel within a few minutes of the area, and I think it's a good spot. I can book you a high-up room if you'd like. You could run the drone from there."

"Sounds good. Send me that address."

CHAPTER 25
PRAGUE CZECH REPUBLIC

Aphid's phone buzzed on his desk, disrupting the peace in his sterile office in the warehouse. *Pavel Brozik.* The specimen collector.

"Yes?"

"They are here, in Prague, sir. Two women and several private security detail in business suits. They look American, maybe government. In the North East. They are in a house in Choceňská. Almost at the north end of the street."

"Wonderful. Thank you, Pavel. Keep me posted. Don't approach them."

CHAPTER 26 SAN JOSE, CALIFORNIA

Dead men don't tell tales, they text.

Pierce froze when he read the text from Alex. His mentor Alex had configured a critical intelligence updates feed to continue in his absence automatically. He preferred to maintain direct communications with Pierce in the field, but occasionally would be called into other tasks and wanted to ensure there was no time lag from information gathered to information disseminated.

Pierce and Kelly donned their tactical gear. Kelly's gloves were measured to fit her hands down to the millimeter; Pierce's boots contained handcuff keys inside a hidden compartment.

Everything was customized, designed, and fitted for the mission. Their radios were a direct line to Mariel in the operations center below HIG. Pierce doubted he needed them, but slid three flashbangs into his body armor pouches anyway. He retrieved two more, placing them into Kelly's.

Their outfits were designed to look casual. Pierce's khaki pants could stretch four times their width, allowing tremendous freedom of movement. The pants also integrated Kevlar at the junction of joints and near vital organs. His blue dress shirt was designed with the same technology.

They only had one lead, and it was David Morris. Aside from being the CEO of Follow-Me, the biggest social media company on Earth, he had amassed a fortune selling what he called 'behavioral metrics' to companies who tailored ads to consumers.

Morris's house was situated abutting a golf course just outside of the city. Pierce and Kelly decided to drive to the opposite side of the golf course and walk across the fairway. They had to either warn him of the approaching danger, get him out of town, or simply persuade his security team to triple down on protection for the evening.

Kelly maneuvered their newly acquired SUV into the driveway of a house they had confirmed was uninhabited on a home-rental vacation website. They exited the vehicle and moved quickly into the backyard.

Pierce retrieved a translucent cord from his shirt collar and placed it in his ear. Kelly did the same. Pierce squeezed the mic button on his wrist.

"We're across the fairway now. Moving."

The HIG command center was located only two floors below where Alex had been murdered. It was staffed with operations personnel that knew their business. The command center always reminded Pierce of a James Bond movie. He never imagined he'd be back on the other side of missions after his fiancée was killed.

"Loud and clear," Mariel's voice came back. "Copy. It looks like the power meter is low right now. Might be an empty house. His travel schedule has him at home, though."

"Got it."

Kelly pried open the rear gate of the house that led to the golf course, and Pierce followed her onto the perfectly manicured grass.

They trotted up to the rear of the CEO's house. Kelly slowed and tucked in behind a low bush. Pierce passed her and held position behind a power box.

"It's dark, but I don't think anyone's home. Not even security."

"Agreed," Pierce said. "Back door."

"Moving," Kelly whispered into her mic.

"Covering."

In a low crouch, Kelly loped to the back gate and used a large sprinkler pipe to volley over the fence. Pierce whirled, scanning for any threats behind them. Satisfied, he crept to the fence and covered Kelly from behind.

Kelly rounded the pool, neared the back door, and immediately changed course. She flanked to her left and knelt behind a brick wall near the large sliding glass door. It led into the largest living room Pierce had ever seen.

"Door's been opened. Pried open," Kelly whispered.

Pierce contemplated the situation for less than a second. "We're going in."

He jumped the fence and raced to Kelly, scouring the area around them while she waited to enter.

After a nod, they both drew silenced Five-seveN pistols, slid the door aside, and moved into the house. Inside of the small sling bag on Pierce's back was a high-output jammer that could shut off any nearby communications device.

"Going dark on communications," Pierce whispered into his mic.

"Copy. Dark."

He reached onto his belt and flipped a small switch, activating it. A short, faint beep sounded in his earpiece, letting him know they had lost communications with HIG. He leaned forward to confirm with Kelly they were going dark on communications, but she was already holding up a thumb in the air.

After a meticulous search through the rooms of the sprawling, luxurious house, they confirmed that no one was home. They found nothing but silence. Pierce and Kelly stood alone in the quiet, dark kitchen.

"Maybe he got the message to get out of town," Kelly offered with a shrug.

Pierce saw a single object on the kitchen counter that seemed to have been tossed there. He retrieved a small, red flashlight from his pocket and aimed it at the object. It was a photograph of David Morris and his wife holding glasses of white wine in front of a small private plane.

"Eclipse 550," Pierce said.

"What's that?"

"It's a private jet. A small one. I used to take these from Jacksonville to Cuba when I was running interviews in Guantanamo."

Pierce shut the jammer off and waited for the beep in his earpiece to let him know his communications with HIG were back online.

"Show me that picture, Kelly."

Kelly slid the photo off the counter and held it out for Pierce. He squeezed his mic button.

"Mariel, write this down. N64651E. Get me everything you can on this tail number. Small aircraft. Should go back to an Eclipse 550."

"Check. Standby."

Kelly eyed the photo under the red light. "This looks like California for sure. Small airport, though."

"Agreed. But there's got to be a thousand of those in California.

Pierce keyed the mic on his wrist. "Update. House was broken into. No sign of any struggle. Might have happened after they left the house."

"Copy, Pierce. That aircraft is registered to a company called Branchfield Holdings. It looks like they do bullshit overseas banking stuff. Registered owner is Kyle Hunt. Lives there in San Jose. I'll keep digging."

"Copy. Sending a photo to you now."

Pierce snapped a photo under the red light, tucked the picture into his back pocket, and sent the image to HIG.

As he clicked off the small flashlight, the entire kitchen erupted in white light coming in from the front yard.

"Someone's here. Front yard."

"Not police, Pierce. I've been listening to every local scanner."

"Down," Pierce ordered in a whisper.

The light shone through the large windows again, scanning the kitchen. Kelly positioned herself behind a counter, and Pierce slid below the window as light cast over him into the dark room. He narrowed his focus into the darkest corner of the room he could find, trying to keep his eyes adjusted to the darkness so he could maneuver.

"Hello!" a voice shouted from next to the kitchen.

A moment passed in silence as Kelly watched Pierce, trying to breathe without making a sound.

"Front door is open!" the voice shouted again.

The bright cone of light shone directly into the next room over.

Neighborhood security, he thought.

Pierce whispered into his mic, "Cover your ears."

He waited a second, then shouted a long, confusing string of words, followed by a HIG phrase.

After two seconds, the light shining into the house slowly lowered to the floor.

He yelled another phrase to ensure they wouldn't get caught up by some trigger-happy security guard.

The light didn't move.

"Drop the light. It's fine," he coaxed.

The metallic ping of the flashlight hitting tile echoed through the giant house.

"Great job! Come on in. You'll notice, immediately, that everything is okay."

Pierce rose and approached the entryway of the house. The security man wore a typical security guard's uniform and appeared to be in his early sixties. Probably an ex-cop.

Pierce extended his hand, and the security man did the same.

"Brent Phillips," Pierce said.

"Good to meet you."

Kelly stayed put. It wouldn't help them if a description of the two of them made it to law enforcement—not some couple dressed in what looked like a Ralph Lauren tactical clothing line.

"I'm...I'm okay?" The security guard spoke in a bewildered tone all too familiar to Pierce.

Pierce rested a hand on the man's shoulder. "All good, man! I was just waiting to get that information about what else you saw here at the house earlier."

"Oh, yes. Gray van. Driver had a beard. Alone. I never saw it before, but it had a sticker, so I didn't call it in."

These neighborhoods paid police extra to keep their villages safe. Each vehicle had stickers on them, indicating those who lived in the neighborhood. Police would avoid giving them tickets and pulling them over, and would even help them with groceries.

"That's great. Great job. And you can just tell me what time that was?"

"Yes. Probably...forty-five minutes ago."

"Thanks so much for ***you're willing to help me*** so much. I appreciate it. It's always one of those things that you notice just like when you can't think of something you wanted to forget and remembering gets harder and harder. Noticing that more and more when we try to remember this wasn't really sure about everything—might just be—***let completely go*** of the entire thing here— and we're all fine. You were going this way, or to your car?"

Pierce gestured to the front door.

"Right. Just to the car. Have a great night."

The security man picked up his flashlight and strolled out the front door.

Pierce closed it softly with a gloved hand and turned the lock.

Kelly stood with a slight smile and whispered, "Nice job, Boss!" with a wink.

Pierce grabbed the mic button on his wrist again. "We need data. Gray minivan, probably around an hour ago in this neighborhood. See if there's any footage from the city. We need to see where he went."

After making it back to the SUV, both of their earpieces activated.

"Guys, I'm looking at this now. Mr. Morris, the CEO of Follow-Me, was college roommates with the owner of the plane. They both dropped out of Yale. The executive security company that is protecting Mr. Morris has protocols for major threats. One of the most common threat responses is to reserve flights on several airlines and have dummy vehicles leave the home at random times, headed in different directions. That's probably what happened tonight. Hopefully, he's out of the house and whoever broke in got there after they left."

"Great," Kelly groaned into her mic. "We've got God knows how many vehicles to chase down. When are the HIG teams arriving? We're going to need them."

"Teams should be suited up in less than two hours. They will have police support; they are all traveling to you under the cover of Federal Agents. Their cover is for a massive drug shipment suspected to leave the harbor tomorrow."

"Fuck," Kelly whispered.

Pierce figured the weight of what they were up against was dawning on her. She was finally coming to the conclusion that they may not make it out of this.

Their earpieces beeped again. "Hey. No need to track down vehicles. I just got a hit. There was a flight plan listed for that aircraft fifty-three minutes ago. Flight from Napa County Airport to Seattle. David Morris owns an ocean-front house in Seattle. This might not be a home run, but this is as solid as leads get. In the meantime, our people are still calling the executive security company to see if they can persuade someone over the phone to get travel information."

"We're heading to Napa. Phone me if anything else comes up."

Pierce turned to Kelly, who was busy chewing on her lip. He placed a hand on her shoulder. She raised her eyes to meet his.

"We're going to Napa. Everything's going to be fine. We'll get him in time."

He only hoped she couldn't tell he was lying

.

CHAPTER 27
PRAGUE CZECH REPUBLIC

There was no way out. If Deidra found the building, she would stop at nothing to destroy everyone in it.

On the drive into the city, Jennifer had found few hotels that offered a view of the area. The tallest hotel in the vicinity of AFI city was The Clarion Congress Hotel.

The two women rode the long escalator into the futuristic looking lobby. Long lines of LED lights gave it the appearance of a spaceship. Deidra spoke to the hotel manager and secured a room on the seventh floor, ensuring that it faced east.

Their security brought the luggage and equipment to the room. Deidra set up the drone equipment, and Jennifer decided to speak to a few local police, take a look around AFI city herself, and see if she could somehow find a building that looked like it was housing a group of international terrorists.

She took one of the security men with her. Being a fluent Czech speaker, Jennifer was apt to gain more information from the locals.

At the Clarion Congress Hotel, Deidra set up an antenna in the window with a suction cup and pulled the small drone from its hard case. She didn't know the first thing about flying the machine, but the young analyst boys at HIG assured her they could operate it from Virginia. Her only job was to plug a computer into the controller's data port and flip the power switch.

She hadn't been on an operation in five years, and it felt good to be back out. She belonged here, not behind a desk. She still dressed the part of director: black slacks, a tan blouse, and a black business blazer. But she'd chosen her running shoes instead of heels.

"Ma'am, please make sure your fingers and hair are nowhere near this thing when we say 'clear.'"

She knew better. Her only grandson, a six-year-old, had flown a tiny drone into her hair the previous Christmas.

After the room was secured, most of the security detail departed, leaving Deidra with her usual security staff of three men.

Two were in the hallway and one was in the kitchen, on his phone. They were great to her and treated every member of her friends and family with kindness she would only expect from close friends.

Deidra sat on the couch and poured steaming coffee into a short, white cup. She waited for the boys at HIG to do whatever technical work they were doing to some update on the drone's software. She knew it had about a twenty-nine-minute flight time, but little else.

She then did something she hadn't done in front of anyone in years. She reached into her tall, leather purse, withdrew a pack of Marlboro Light cigarettes, and tore the wrapper off. She lit a cigarette, leaned back, and blew the smoke to the ceiling. The HIG team was moving into Prague within the hour, and she would be able to direct them into the hornet's nest.

In the event she found the place where these files were stored, she would have a mountain of data that would also reveal who could have exposed HIG publicly, but didn't. That perplexed her the most. Whoever stole the video from Pierce's iPad had to understand there was at least some kind of agency involved, and the video contained several clues to the rightful owner, should it ever get lost. She hoped the incidents were a coincidence, that the encryption using computer vision hadn't been cracked. She took another drag on the cigarette to redirect her train of thought.

Her computer beeped.

Incoming call from HIG 23948.

The boys are ready.

The security man stepped from the kitchen and said, "Ma'am, I'll be outside while you're on the call."

He excused himself. Deidra tapped the answer

key, and an encryption key ran through a small series of numbers before the call connected.

The HIG technical experts chimed in; both seemed thrilled to be doing this mission and probably excited to talk to Deidra.

"Ma'am?"

"Hey, guys. Thanks for the help here. What can I do?"

"Yes, ma'am. Of course. We just need you to attach a battery pack to the bottom of the drone and hold down the red button on the front of it until you hear a short beep."

Deidra did as they instructed. "What's this button do?"

"It's a self-destruct button."

"What? What the hell do you mean?"

"No, no. Not like that, Ma'am. If it's not recovered, or you decide to fly it until it dies, we can just leave it, and it will destroy all the data inside. It won't, like, blow up or anything."

"Got it. Say that next time you tell an old woman she's pushing a self-destruct button, please."

"I thought you were, like, twenty-eight, Ma'am."

Deidra decided to let them suffer through a short silence.

"Uh, ma'am, so the next thing you need to do is open the window and hold it out as far as you can from the building in a horizontal position. We can see the camera and all the controls here. It will have about a one-second delay, but it won't affect us much at all. We loaded the necessary Software Radio into the drone as well. We just had to tell it what to listen for."

"What is it going to listen for?"

"A few things. We're going to get great video, and send that to the team in Prague, and we'll get other data like Bluetooth signals, Wi-Fi signals, jammers, and most types of communications equipment. We can see through walls in a way, and if a building *should* be unoccupied, and it has lots of signals coming out of it, we are going to flag that building. Hopefully, we find something."

"Great. Thank you. I hope that you only find one of these. We don't have time for a search at this point."

"Ready when you are, ma'am."

Deidra walked to the window and slid it open about six inches, just enough to get the drone through.

She held out her arm as far as she could and opened her hand, letting the heavy little drone rest on her palm.

"Ready."

"Clear. Three, two, one. Taking off, ma'am."

With a noisy buzz, the four propellers spun to life in a way that startled her, and the drone flew off much faster than she had imagined.

"Looks good from here," Deidra said.

"Okay, Director. We are live. No issues. We should have the area mapped in about fifteen minutes. If we need more time, I'll keep it in the air until it's dead."

"Thanks, guys. I'm signing off. Keep me posted on my company cell."

Her posture relaxed with a sigh. Answers would come. She had scrambled every asset she knew, called in favors from people who probably didn't want to hear from her again. Whoever was behind this needed to be found and wiped off the face of the earth.

Deidra walked past the sitting area, where her coffee was still warm, to the kitchen to call Jennifer. The moment she stepped onto the tile of the small kitchen, a heavy thud came from the hallway.

As it registered in her mind, she sidestepped immediately to be out of firing range from the door and approached it from the side. She came within about two feet of it, straining to listen, and watching closely under the door for movement. A black iPad slid under the door slowly.

It was powered on, a video chat active on the screen.

Deidra pushed the iPad away from the door with her foot, and, before she picked it up, recognized the horror on the screen.

Jennifer sat in a green armchair, an old brick wall behind her. A larger person wearing a full-face mask stood next to her. Ropes tied her arms to the chair; the man held a submachine gun. The barrel in Jennifer's mouth. Jennifer didn't look at the camera. She likely knew it would cause more of the fear they intended to incite.

Deidra stopped breathing.

A robotic voice coming through the speakers on the iPad shattered the silence of the live video.

“Deidra Collins. Director of the HIG.”

The voice sent chills through her body. It was clinical and unreadable. The voice of Hell.

“If there are no agents with you in the room, knock on the door three times. If an agent is in the room, knock once. If you move for a weapon, Jennifer dies. If a sound leaves your mouth, Jennifer dies. Nod your head.”

Deidra nodded. She gritted her teeth, trying to keep from screaming, crying. She began to shake.

“Good,” the voice continued.

“Knock on the door as instructed. Jennifer has three seconds to live unless compliance occurs.”

She flicked her hand forward and rapped on the door, three times.

“Open the door, Deidra Collins. We assure you that no one will be harmed. We only want to meet with you.”

Deidra stepped toward the door and managed to grab a small kitchen knife off the counter. She gripped the knife in her right hand and turned the silver door handle with her left hand to pull the door open an inch. Whoever it was, was going to die. If it was a group, the first one to come into the room would die.

She stepped back, set down the iPad, and leaned forward on the balls of her feet.

The door swung open, and she readied herself to take on whatever came through the doorway.

A flash of light erupted from behind the door. Then nothing.

CHAPTER 28

NAPA, CALIFORNIA

Trent sped up Interstate 680 toward Napa.

He had broken into David Morris's house easier than he thought possible. The alarm system had been connected to a phone line that was exposed to the exterior of the house. It took less than a second to clip the wire. Surely a man who has that much money wouldn't forego online camera systems unless he knew they *did* something that no one else knew about.

Within about ten minutes in the house, Trent encountered what he needed. On the refrigerator, he saw a photograph of the man and his wife in front of a small plane. He ran the tail number through a free and public app on his phone that anyone could use to track aircraft, and immediately found his target's location.

Before leaving the house, he found a laptop on the living room coffee table that seemed to have been discarded in a hurry. The bedrooms looked as though someone had packed and left quickly as well. Trent took the laptop, placed it into a faraday bag, and got back into his van, speeding toward Napa.

He once worked for an executive protection company before, and he was always impressed with the complex, detailed security reaction protocols they memorized to protect the 'asset.' One thing was well known in these circles, however—no matter how smart these plans were, you could never underestimate the stupidity of the 'asset.' These poor bastards had probably spent a hundred grand tonight setting up decoy trips, buying plane tickets to wherever, and having a dozen or so vehicles pull into the garage and leave. But the 'asset' would always fuck it up.

Tonight, he was grateful for that.

After driving for almost an hour and a half, he pulled into the only airport he found in the federal flight plans for the aircraft. This plane had returned here after each trip. The airport became his only hope, and his last chance to complete this mission. He had no idea when this plane was going to take off, and he contemplated calling in a bomb threat to the airport to stall the CEO's departure.

In bootcamp, he learned patience. In special warfare units, he learned that patience *wins*.

The Napa county airport was a tiny airport by most accounts, housing only small planes, mostly private jets. It was dark when he arrived.

As he drove the van into the parking lot, Trent shoved the stolen laptop into his backpack along with three pistols. He kept his favorite pistol on his belt, however. A Ruger MK IV with a short silencer. That weapon had gotten him out of a lot of tough times where quiet was the only option. He had even used it in a house full of otherwise sleeping people.

Trent counted three cars in the parking lot—all parked facing the building to the left of the main terminal.

He pulled the car in without any lights on and crept to a stop beside them. He slipped out into the darkness, went to the back of the van, and popped a large case open, revealing his matte black hunting crossbow. His pistol may have been quiet, but this thing was no more than a whisper. He packed his gear, readied an arrow in the weapon, and threw the sling of the crossbow across his body, letting it hang in front of him.

With his backpack on, he slipped between the hoods of the vehicles and a sheet metal wall. These assholes may have brought extra protection tonight. It was a shame. He never liked killing veteran special ops. They deserved more dignity, but if the mission needed it, he would.

He slid between the bumpers of the cars and the metal wall, running his gloved hand along the hood of each vehicle to check if it had arrived recently. Only one was warm. A black Mercedes Benz.

If he brought his wife, that's a maximum of two security if they rode in the back seat.

He made his way to the end of the parking wall. Light spilled from the windows on a door to his left when he reached the corner. He turned left and pulled out his phone. He opened the camera app, lifted only the lens to the glass window, and took seven photos.

Trent pulled his body back to the wall, careful not to hit the crossbow on the metallic, corrugated wall at his back. The photos showed a blurry plane identical to the one in the photograph, an empty hangar, and a man standing about three feet from the door. His back was to the camera, but he was definitely wearing a cheap suit.

One security, check.

Time was scarce, so he set a one-minute timer on his phone, turned the volume to maximum, and set the timer alert tone to a ringtone. He removed his glove, slid the phone into it to block the light from the screen, and placed it face down to the right of the opening of the door. As the phone's timer counted down, Trent backed into a small, dark corner which made him blend in with the solid black of the night. He took his remaining time to regulate his breathing and rehearse his next move.

In about forty seconds, the timer began chiming a stupid ringtone consisting of beeps, xylophone sounds, and birds chirping.

Trent adjusted his squatting position and raised the crossbow to the door. He only had one shot, but his draw from the holster with his silenced .22 was less than half a second should something go wrong.

For the first time in a long time, Trent felt something rare: his heart rate increased. He was excited.

The security man's chubby face appeared in the window, searching for the source of the sound. He searched for much longer through the window than Trent had envisioned. Finally, the doorknob creaked, and he extended his upper body through the door to investigate. The slightly fat security guy had drawn his weapon, but years without combat—without killing—had taught him to conceal it by his right leg so as not to scare anyone.

Pussy.

As the man in the piece of shit suit turned his head, Trent sent a silent arrow—equipped with one-inch razor blades at the tip for hunting—through the man's face.

His mouth sagged, his eyes fixed in lifeless state of shock as he fell the rest of the way through the doorway.

Trent stood and immediately readied another razor arrow into the crossbow and touched the pistol on his leg to ensure his muscle memory wouldn't fail if he needed it in the next thirty seconds.

He stepped on the dead–or dying–security man and leapt through the door. The CEO and his wife stood in front of a pile of bags in the center of the hangar near the plane. Both of them froze in fear as panic overtook them. Trent approached them as fast as he could, knowing no secondary security staff would take a shot if he got close to them, much less with a crossbow aimed at the man's head.

The CEO spoke up, stepping slightly in front of his wife. "Take - take the plane. It's yours. We don't want any–"

Trent held up a finger. The CEO fell silent.

Trent spoke quickly and quietly.

"You say one word you both die now. Nod if you understand."

The couple, trembling, both nodded.

"Is there another security here? Another E.P.?"

Both shook their heads. They didn't look at each other or hesitate. A good sign. Trent remembered these signals from his days going house to house in Afghanistan asking if families had rockets or bombs in their homes. Those were the two signs he looked for.

He looked the CEO in the eyes and pushed the cold silencer into the soft skin of his wife's neck.

CHAPTER 29

PRAGUE, CZECH REPUBLIC

Deidra blinked back into consciousness. The smell of aftershave lingered in the air. She was still in her hotel room. An older man in a fancy suit with light skin sat opposite her in the sitting area. Two large men wearing suits and masks stood behind him against the wall, each of them with an assault rifle pointed at her. She felt pain in her neck and chest. She glanced down and saw a small circle of blood from where a taser prong had pierced her skin.

The older man spoke up before she had a chance to assemble a thought. "Deidra, if you speak a single word these men *will* kill you. Understand?"

She nodded, blinking, still trying to regain her thoughts. His accent was almost Canadian. She couldn't place it.

"Here's how this will work. I'd like this to be a civilized conversation. I'll act like a gentleman, and I'd like you to be the same charming, polite woman that you always are. I'm going to allow you to speak. The men behind me don't speak English, and I know for a fact you don't speak a word of Polish. They can't hear you anyway."

Deidra appraised the men holding rifles. Each of them had equipped themselves with high-end earbuds.

"They are listening to Polish music. It's shit, but they don't know better. However, if these men see my arms leave the chair, or if I make any movements without giving them a signal first, they will shoot you immediately in the forehead, and prevent me from doing whatever it is you tell me to do with your manipulation tactics. Do you understand this as I've said it?"

Her jaw clenched in rage as she offered a curt nod.

The man's hands were firmly clasped onto the arms of the chair in front of her. "You can speak, Deidra."

"Yes. I understand."

"Good. I have no intention of hurting you. I can assure you. I'm no monster."

"What do you want from me, mister...?"

"Please, just call me Aphid."

Deidra had heard the name before. She scrambled internally to figure out where she had heard it. Maybe she'd seen it somewhere. It was about a week ago. Where the hell had she seen it?

"Why Aphid? Childhood nickname?"

He laughed. His hands stayed bolted to the arms of the chair. His words were carefully chosen and unhurried. "Aphids have always fascinated me. When I was a boy, I learned about them. I think they are the most adaptive insect on Earth. They're born pregnant, and they don't have wings unless they need them. Aphids are expert fighters, and even have skills that resemble Jiu Jitsu. What I most enjoyed learning was that when a group of them is threatened, they produce soldiers to protect them. The soldiers they give birth to even have different DNA from the other aphids, with the sole life purpose of sacrificing themselves to save the others."

"I certainly never knew those things."

Aphid leaned in closer. "Your friend is fine. Jennifer is a lovely woman. She'll not be hurt."

After a moment of silence, he spoke again. "Are you familiar with MK ULTRA?"

"Yes." Her stomach began to sink. Another conspiracy theorist.

"What are your thoughts about MK ULTRA, Deidra?"

She considered for a moment and decided to simply tell him the truth. She spoke slowly through the fog that was still clearing from her mind. "I think, in a time of extreme uncertainty, the government realized that the war of minds was more powerful than nuclear weapons. In an arms race to control the mind, they allowed some deranged morons to run the show. It got out of hand, more morons came into the picture, and medical doctors violated every ethical rule of medicine. No one was punished, and people were hurt. A *lot* of people."

Aphid gave her a warm smile. “I couldn't have said it better. But one of the worst cases was underreported. It took place in Canada. Do you remember?”

“I—think so. Montreal?”

“Precisely.” He smiled. “In Montreal, there was a doctor who did some horrible things. Some of the people there even lost decades of memories, could no longer walk straight, unable to function as adults; they had to wear diapers.”

Deidra struggled to identify his personality profile based on his words. He spoke in a way that left little to determine. Only his facial expressions seemed to reveal his true feelings. He was probably lying about not killing her. Every scenario she could think of ended up with her dead; even if she were able to use Tradecraft on him, and had him keep his hands on the chair, she'd be able to do nothing.

Aphid crossed his legs and sat back in his chair. His movement made her anxious. She worried the men wouldn't misinterpret his actions and kill her.

“Would you like some tea?”

“No, thank you,” Deidra said.

"Let me be completely honest with you here." He adjusted in the seat. "I was eight years old when my mother returned from a hospital stay in Montreal. It was 1956. I was a little boy and didn't understand why my mom acted different. She began wetting herself the first day. By the end of the first week, she had hit herself in the face so many times that her nose was permanently disfigured. My father tried to figure out what was wrong and received no help from the hospital. She spoke like a two-year-old—couldn't form simple sentences."

"I'm so sorry." Deidra meant it.

Aphid continued. "It was a month or so into it all when my father left. He was a little coward, but I didn't know it then. I continued to go to school and take care of her. *No one* would help. I *knew* that when I spoke to her, she was still there. I could see it in her eyes, you know? People from the hospital came to check on her after several months. They wouldn't let me in the bedroom with them while they spoke to her. The following day, I awoke, and she had disappeared. While I slept, she had somehow gone outside, walked onto the freeway, and thrown herself in front of a truck."

Deidra knew Aphid saw *her* as being responsible for this, and she imagined the things he might have in mind. She needed out. But there was no way to overpower these men.

"Mr. Aphid, I'm deeply sorry. I never heard about this. I can't imagine the horrors."

"I wouldn't *like* you to imagine them. With no parents, the nearest relative of mine was an uncle in Ukraine. He was a wealthy man with no time for kids, and I was raised by his housekeeper. I learned a lot from my uncle. I'm wealthy now because of him."

"What do you want with me? Why am I here?"

"America never stopped this obsessive pursuit of psychological dominance. Of course, the MK ULTRA project and others came to an end, but the pursuit of this never stopped. It has gotten to a point where the country, and any other country that seems to befriend America has come to a point of celebrating ignorance, idolizing social media, and championing self-absorption."

"I agree with you, Aphid, but—"

"I'll finish if you don't mind, Deidra." His voice was a razor blade.

Deidra closed her eyes and nodded.

"The reason you're here is because this didn't start with MK ULTRA, it began with your organization, *named* after the first psychological manipulation technique to control political leaders in Europe. An endeavor to manipulate political leaders for whatever your group deems 'safe' for humanity." Aphid's eyes narrowed. "HIG. *Hand-In-Glove.* A method to bypass the people, dismiss the democracy, and control the Earth."

Deidra's jaw dropped as the pointed words came from his mouth. Aphid took her expression as an invitation to continue. "I intend to stop this. And stopping something like this cannot be done with a petition, a campaign, or even by exposing you all on television. A massive *event* is the only thing that changes culture in America. Civil war, Pearl Harbor, and the attacks in New York."

"You're planning such an event, I assume?"

Her skin crawled. Her breaths came in short bursts as her muscles trembled in her chest.

"You're a black woman."

Deidra made no effort to respond. She thought of Pierce and Kelly. They were the last hope.

"How many thousands sat in the white area of the bus before Rosa Parks did? It took an *event* to get media attention. The media took hold of the small event that eventually led to changes in public policies. The policy changes led to gradual social changes, and even today, your country is more obsessed with race than ever before. Has *anything* changed?"

Deidra stared into the man's eyes. Willing his heart to stop. Willing him to choke to death in front of her. If she stood any chance of escape, it would be during a move, if they decided to move her at all.

He reached forward, taking his hand off the chair, and took a sip of tea. The men behind Aphid held their weapons still. She worked to discover the signal he gave them. She wondered for a moment if there *was* no signal—if he was bluffing. He sipped his tea and gazed out the window.

"An event changes things. The grander the event, the more significant the change, Deidra. If the world is to live in peace, the world needs to see the potential hell your techniques create. Small events can change countries. I intend to change the world. The world deserves peace. People have died for good things throughout history. This is no different.

"Tomorrow, the entire world will see Hell, and they will know *you* created it."

CHAPTER 30
NAPA, CALIFORNIA

On the drive to Napa, Kelly made peace with the fact that this might be the final day of her life.

The feel of body armor sent her mind back to training at HIG only a few months prior.

Kelly stood in the HIG training compound, slid her body armor over her head, loaded up with magazines, and stepped into a four- foot, white circle in the middle of a large training warehouse that smelled heavily of lemon-scented antiseptic. The warehouse contained replicas of city streets, apartment buildings, cars, and even a village street in Iraq.

Every student carried a Glock loaded with training ammunition that shot small, pink projectiles made of wax and paint. They hurt like hell.

"You're not to step outside of the circle or kneel. Remain in the circle. Keep your weapon concealed until you need to use it, or you see a threat emerging." Her instructor had repeated the same instructions to each member of the class.

A black hood was pulled over her head. In front of her, a group of actors wearing paintball face masks would play their roles in a different simulated scenario each time the hood was placed on a trainee's head. Some scenarios were dangerous, and the people in front of you would have weapons. Some were peaceful and had no violence. Sometimes the actors would all be peaceful, and then one of them would pull a gun and try to kill you.

Each scenario lasted about three minutes, and Kelly would have to react within that time to ensure she wasn't killed, and to terminate the threat.

She stood as the black hood covered her head, reeking of gunpowder and sweat.

World-class operators had shown her everything from espionage tradecraft and lockpicking, to gunfighting and countersurveillance.

When the hood was ripped off of her head, a man sat at a table in front of her. A handgun rested on the table before him.

Behind him, a man came around a corner with a rifle and began raising it.

Kelly fired, hitting him directly in the face with three shots. He fell to the ground.

The man at the table was already reaching for the gun. Kelly promptly reoriented her pistol and emptied three rounds into the man's upper chest, and one directly in the center of his face. He fell to the ground. A loud beep sounded to indicate the scenario was over. The instructors scrambled to their feet to recreate another scene as the hood was lowered again over Kelly's head.

It was an endless string of scenarios for eleven hours with only a few breaks for the bathroom and water. She imagined the welts covering the instructors' bodies at the end of the day and felt horrible for adding to the wounds.

Every movement they made in training was recorded on dozens of cameras. Kelly and the other students would sit with the instructors for hours, dissecting video of every muscle movement and correcting every mistake they made. None of them were permitted to make any kind of facial expression while they went through tactical scenarios. Since emotions and facial expressions were tied so closely together, facial expressions could trigger emotional reactions to situations in real life. If you grimaced, frowned, clenched a jaw, or reacted in any other way, it meant you weren't internally calm. Kelly learned the reverse was also true; facial expressions could *create* emotions as much as they could identify them.

That morning, Kelly and the other students had watched a confidential video from a special operations unit in Afghanistan. She watched in amazement as one of the men got shot in the leg and exhibited no facial expression. He only continued moving forward, shooting, fighting.

Terminators, she had thought.

Pierce's voice broke into the memory, binging her back to the present.

"I think I'll park about a quarter-mile out. The HIG teams should get here in about fifty minutes.

We can get there on foot from wherever we put the vehicle."

"What are we going to do?" Kelly had faith in her training, but still felt like she'd been tasked with fighting a giant.

Pierce turned to Kelly. "Find him. Talk to him. Kill him. Avoid dying."

"I'll take point on this if you think I should. You're more experienced and you stand a better chance at taking him out or using Tradecraft on him if I get hit first," Kelly said.

He nodded, his jaw clenched. She thought about his tragedy. Kelly rolled her eyes at herself. She knew she should have worded that differently.

She wondered what he'd been through. The missions, the assignments he'd seen, the heartbreak he had to have experienced losing a fiancée. She adjusted herself in the seat and pulled out a tablet containing maps and plans of the airport.

"We should be there in eight minutes. The private jets are usually kept in hangars just south of the main terminal building. This is a tiny community airport. The whole airport is closed now. Two runways, and it looks like we will have several potential hangars to search. If he decides to take them into a plane, we're going to have to figure that out."

"If they're in the air, we will go after them. I don't know how, but we will get it done," Pierce said.

Kelly snapped her M4 rifle to an elastic sling hanging from the shoulder of her body armor. Each of them had three magazines of M4 ammunition attached to their armor and three magazines for their handguns.

Tucked into a horizontal pocket on the back of their armor, Pierce and Kelly each had military-grade programmable radios for comms. A small first aid kit was attached to the underside of their armor.

Pierce pulled the vehicle to the side about a quarter mile east of the airport. This industrial part of the city was vacant this late at night. Pierce stood at the back of the vehicle in the darkness and snapped his rifle into a sling running through his armor. Each of them had an FBI windbreaker rolled into a side cargo pocket and a set of FBI credentials tucked into their armor.

Both switched on their radios and watched the green screen power up. They slid the radios into the long, rectangular pouches and pushed the earpieces back into their ears.

Pierce touched his mic button. "We're online. Going into the airport now."

Mariel's soothing voice came through the radio. "I see you on the map here. Teams should be there within an hour if you need them."

"Thanks, Mariel. We are going in now. If the plane takes off, this is going to evolve into a much more complex scenario."

They crept in the unlit street through one gate, leapt over a fence, and stepped onto airport property in less than ten minutes.

In the darkness before them were rows of silent, unlit hangars, with a larger hangar closest to the runway. The breeze whipped across the runway, rattling the huge steel doors of the nearby hangar, the only sound they could hear. Everything was black, silent. Hugging the walls of the hangars, they made their way to the hangar closest to the runway.

Kelly saw a strip of light emanating from the hangar's side door and reached back to stop

Pierce. She pointed to the light. Pierce gave her a quick nod. They rounded the back of the hangar, stopping every few steps to listen.

Nothing.

Kelly kept her eye out for motion-sensing lights and cameras. Nothing. She took another step, and felt a crunch under her boot. A loud, but muffled, *pop* came from under her foot. She picked her heel up to find she had crushed a small lightbulb, like a brake light from a car.

Pierce tapped her and ran from where they stood to a shadowed area next to a large green power conversion box at the corner of the building closest to them. Kelly trailed close behind.

Any time they made a sound that could reveal their location, their first priority was what her instructors called 'getting off the 'x"—an immediate departure from where an enemy might have heard a sound, likely the first place they would begin looking. Or shooting.

They sat crouched, rifles pointed at a door beside a loading area that led to the hangar. Kelly cursed under her breath, flipped off her safety, and waited. She had screwed up in front of one of the very few men she admired.

"Sorry," she finally let out.

"I've done way worse," Pierce replied.

They waited for another minute until Pierce spoke again. "Let's get in there."

Kelly moved ahead to the rear door they had been watching. She placed a gloved hand around the knob and twisted it slowly. It was an unlit back room connected to the hangar. Without night vision, she had the option of going in dark or using the light mounted on her M4 to illuminate the room. Each of the choices carried risk. Deciding on caution, she went in dark.

Pierce tapped her right shoulder, indicating he was ready. She used her elbow to open the door as slowly as she could. The small room leading to the hangar was quiet. She moved across the room to a nearby corner and waited for Pierce to follow. It stunk of cigarettes.

This has got to lead to the hangar.

Pierce tapped her shoulder again. She raised the barrel of her short rifle and began quietly moving toward a corner that led to the hangar.

Crouched around the corner in the shadows, was a figure of a man. She didn't have time to react. The barrel of her gun jerked so violently toward the ceiling that it came out of her hands. The man yanked her forward into him by the neck of her body armor, with his gun leveled over Kelly's shoulder and pointed at Pierce. She was face to face with the killer they'd been tracking.

"Gun down. Now." The man spoke in a calm, controlled tone as he ripped Kelly's earpiece out of her ear. "Pull out the earpiece," he ordered Pierce.

Hearing protection covered his ears, a white cord running under them. Music blasted through the headphones.

Fuck.

The man began backing up, hugging Kelly close to him. His beard scratched her face.

He's using me as a fucking shield.

She heard Pierce's rifle smack the floor.

"Take the pistol out with your left hand. No one has to die here, dude." As the man spoke, it became clear where the cigarette smell was coming from.

She went through her options. She could try and draw her pistol–he would kill Pierce. She could bite him in the neck–he would incapacitate or kill her. If she kneed him in the groin, he would back up, and she could attempt to control his barrel while she drew her pistol.

"Great job. Put it on the floor with your rifle, take four steps toward me, and turn around–hands interlocked on the back of your head."

She heard Pierce's pistol clack onto the concrete floor. He had obviously seen the headphones; he hadn't said a word. Her heart raced faster with each breath.

With the man holding her to him, she had little room to move. His arm was blocking access to her pistol. He ripped the pistol from her holster and tucked it into the back of his waistband. He took another step back, pulling Kelly with him, keeping a gun trained on Pierce, and began unbuckling her belt.

CHAPTER 31
YORKTOWN, VIRGINIA

Mariel had run the operations division for seven years. Tonight, she sat in the command center and wondered if there would be an America tomorrow.

She couldn't reach Deidra and was actively listening to Pierce Reston and Kelly Kennedy being disarmed at gunpoint.

The HIG team was fifty-five minutes away from the Napa airport, but they may not have that long.

She had dialed Deidra's laptop and satcom phone over thirty times now, and Jennifer's cell had disappeared from the tracker.

Mariel called the HIG team leader en route to Napa.

"Go."

"ETA to Napa Airport?"

"Fifty-eight minutes now, ma'am."

"How far are you from the Santa Clara Valley Medical Center?"

Mariel heard him ask one of the team members to look it up. After a brief pause, he replied, "Looks like about four minutes."

In her entire time at HIG, Mariel had never sanctioned the use of HIG Enhanced Influence on an innocent civilian.

"Head there now. Medical helicopter is on the roof. Have team two continue driving to the airport in case there's an issue. I don't care who you need to use Tradecraft on, take the helicopter."

"Copy that. Turn around! Head to the hospital," Mariel heard him yell to the driver.

"We have two pilots on this team, ma'am. We can probably be there in thirty to forty minutes if we take that chopper."

CHAPTER 32

NAPA, CALIFORNIA

The sound of Kelly's belt being unbuckled echoed in the small, dark room. Pierce's jaw clenched painfully as he listened.

Trent took her belt off and looped it over Kelly's head, tightening it around her neck. Pierce knew Trent couldn't hear them, but he wasn't ready to see this happen. His blood was on fire. His hands shook.

"Here's how this will work. Pierce, you get in front and lead me through those double doors into the hangar. Kelly, you stay an arm's length behind me. If I feel the slightest movement in any direction, both of you die immediately. I obviously can't hear your hypnosis shit. Nod your head if you understand."

Pierce saw Kelly nod her head and did the same. Kelly didn't deserve this. She hadn't completed training. Another woman in his life would again be killed by a bullet, likely him by the end of the evening.

Pierce walked ahead of the man towing Kelly by the neck behind him and pushed on the left of the double doors. As it opened, light flooded the dark hallway, and Pierce immediately recognized the plane from the photograph in David Morris's kitchen.

The hangar was a tall building meant to hold much larger planes. It was warm, and the smell reminded Pierce of an auto shop, with gasoline lacing the air. The plane was backed into the hangar, with both broad white doors slid open.

To Pierce's left stood two folding tables with computers on them. What he saw behind the tables shook him to the core.

David Morris and his wife, Elanor, were tied up and on their knees. Their legs were secured with zip ties wrapped around the calf and thigh, preventing them from extending their legs. They both wore hearing protection and several layers of silver industrial tape covered their mouths.

David's silver hair protruded from under the hearing muffs, and his wife's slim frame slouched in terror beside him.

"Behind the table," Trent shouted to Pierce, his headphones making him speak louder.

Pierce walked the short distance to the tables, his hands in the air. He surveyed everything on the table. A pen, a yellow legal pad, two laptops, and a satellite communications antenna on a tripod pointed at the giant open doorway of the hangar.

Trent brought Kelly around the table and positioned her next to Pierce before removing the belt from her throat.

"One sound and you're both dead. I don't like killing our kind, but I damn sure will. If you understand, nod your head."

Trent retrieved a duffel bag from beside a tool chest and produced a roll of silver tape along with a large bundle of plastic zip ties. He kept his distance and slid them across the table in front of Kelly, keeping his weapon leveled at her head.

"Pierce, on your knees, just like these two." He gestured to the bound couple beside them.

Pierce schemed. He imagined which tools he could get from the tool chest behind them, all the things he could do with that pen. Any irregular movement would cause Kelly to die. He cursed himself, longing for a drink.

Trent ordered Kelly to bind Pierce in a similar fashion to the wealthy couple using the zip ties, and he could tell she tried to make them as loose as possible. Trent forced her to tighten them almost to the point of cutting off circulation.

With his limbs bound, his mouth covered in layers of tape, Pierce watched as Trent bound Kelly as well, noting that he was careful while placing the tape on her hair. That was a promising sign.

Pierce shifted on his knees. The bound couple beside him remained hunched in fear, Kelly eyed Trent with hatred. Pierce continued devising a plan. With everyone silenced by layers of tape, Trent removed his hearing protection and walked to the table in front of Pierce.

"They can't hear me," Trent whispered, motioning to the couple tied up beside Pierce. "Here's the deal. I'm not removing your tape, but I need you to convince them that they have a lot to lose and all I need this man to do is upload some video file to his social media system. I need him to make it go viral and prevent it from being deleted. It's on this thumb drive."

Trent placed a small, black thumb drive onto the table in front of Pierce.

"That's all they need to do. If you can't convince them, I'm going to start by shooting his wife, do you understand? Upload. Viral. No deleting." Trent slid the pen and legal pad across the table to Pierce.

Pierce nodded. He blinked away a thought of what the video may contain—what this video was capable of. If he tried to destroy the thumb drive, there would likely be a backup; if he attempted to do anything, the video upload would continue next to his dead body. He frantically ran through scenarios in his head. He complied, biding his time.

Trent leaned toward Pierce.

"I'm going to cut the zip ties on your hands. Keep them on the table. If they go under the table, your little girlfriend dies. Take the pen, don't make a single sound, and write down the instructions for Mr. Morris here. Make him understand. Save his wife's life, Pierce."

Hearing this man say his name brought his blood to a boil.

Trent leaned across the table.

"Turn around."

Pierce wiggled to his left. The older man beside him was worth more than just about anyone in the country. Pierce had seen him on television. He'd always looked powerful on TV, and now he resembled a helpless child. His eyes begged for help.

The laptops were opened on the table and connected to a set of large speakers. Pierce wondered why the speakers were necessary, determining that Trent would likely use whatever the video contained on all of them.

> *He's going to test this video on the CEO and his wife. Whatever it contains, David Morris is not going to make it out of here alive.*

Trent pulled a gray knife from a black, plastic sheath on his belt and leaned over to cut the plastic ties from Pierce's hands. Pierce twisted to get a closer look at him. He smelled like cigarettes and soap. A large, grotesque scar split the skin above Trent's right ear. Pierce eyed the scar for a moment, mentally rehearsing a plan.

A sharp tug later, and his hands were free.

Trent walked around the table, gripped Kelly by the shoulder of her body armor, and slid her around like a rag doll in front of the table. He positioned a brown, plastic shopping bag over her head.

"I've done this a hundred times in Afghanistan. She's got about five minutes in there."

He pointed to the pen and legal pad on the table.

"Get it done."

As Pierce wrote the instructions from Trent as fast as he could to David Morris, David nodded his head wildly in acceptance.

Trent punched a number on his phone and held it to his ear. After a minute passed, he clenched his jaw and ended the call.

"Fuck."

Trent' attention darted back to Pierce. The CEO was still nodding his head.

Trent examined what Pierce had written. The instructions were clear and precisely what Trent had asked him to write.

Satisfied, Trent came around and clipped the zip ties on the back of the CEO's hands, freeing them to do his work.

The terrified CEO looked to his wife, sharing an expression of sadness and fear with her. He picked the thumb drive up off the table and inserted it into the laptop. As the download to the laptop began, he leaned across the table and eyed the screen to ensure it was processing.

Trent about-faced again, yanked out his phone, and dialed.

Pierce seized the pen and wrote a second message for the CEO as fast as his hands could move.

'Play 3,000 Hz max volume NOW.'

CHAPTER 33

PRAGUE, CZECH REPUBLIC

If she moved, she'd be shot. Deidra stared at the man before her. This man had set his sights upon destroying the world, and hers had been spent trying to save it. She bowed forward and poured a cup of tea. As she settled back into the chair, a new sense of calm fell over her.

"Mister Aphid, have you ever heard of The Pledge of Allegiance?"

Aphid eyed her with an uncompassionate stare of amusement. "It's what's called a loyalty oath. Many countries have them, but America forces children to stand up and say it repetitively, much like the communist countries you've fought against for almost a century. Children say it without understanding it. Adults say it to convince themselves they are brave and patriotic."

Deidra sipped her tea with a feeling of serenity that surprised her. She could see a hint of concern on the old man's face. He must have noticed her shift in demeanor.

"I agree," Deidra said. "We *don't* teach the children to understand it, only to memorize it. Our country was founded on the pursuit of happiness. Our founding fathers made mistakes, but they were good men who were deeply concerned with the happiness and individual freedoms of everyone who inhabited the Earth."

Aphid's head tilted slightly, indicating curiosity. Deidra continued. "It's the final five words of the Pledge that truly sum up what I'm talking about—liberty and justice for all. It means everyone, *not* just the citizens of the United States."

With an amused expression, Aphid leaned forward, keeping his hands on the arm of the chair.

"Your country gives liberty by overthrowing regimes, killing, then backing out to let some new agency come into power, usually one that is even more violent than the one you removed from control."

Deidra's voice lowered. She spoke in a smooth, even tone.

"It's the pursuit. And I'm willing to do what I need to do. Our country isn't as compelling as some of the things most people wouldn't remember seeing the way the loudest memory could come back and feel like it shouldn't with the export of *weapons* and finally notice the ***arms*** can no longer move, completely stuck in a place and time, here, with me, I think it's easy to let that get completely into the deepest parts of...*you're mine*...just relax."

His face twisted. He wasn't very suggestible. His eyes shot up with his jaw clenched in fury, his eyes widened with rage. His focus shifted to his hands, looking down at them resting on the arms of the chair. He jerked his shoulders, trying to get his arms to cooperate.

"It's okay to give the signal now not to shoot to your men, I think we both of us can never get all the way back to the end of the roads are so blocked here with traffic piling up to remember the moment you're here right now, Aphid."

His face softened, his fingers slackened, and his hand lifted from the arm of the chair. He struggled; his gray eyebrows shot downward in a flash of anger. He stared at his arm, willing it to move. His elbow shot outward off the arm of the chair. The men behind him raised their rifles. Deidra heard the safety switches release. She vaulted from her chair and slid across the coffee table as the room erupted in deafening shots and bright muzzle flashes.

Justice for all.

CHAPTER 34
NAPA, CALIFORNIA

The CEO saw the note and nodded once. He immediately turned to the laptop and searched for '3,000 Hz sound loud.'

He scrolled to find a video with a thumbnail showing a soundwave. Before clicking it, the CEO opened the volume controls. The speakers were already at maximum volume.

Trent spun around and jammed his finger onto his phone screen again, terminating another unanswered call.

"What the fuck are you two doing?"

The CEO didn't break stride and clicked the video. The page loaded and a black rectangle appeared where the video should have been.

A nightmare appeared before them—a loading icon.

As the circle spun on the screen, Trent marched to the table and snatched the laptop. He spun it around and saw the loading video.

"What the f—"

The sound was ear-splitting, filling the entire hangar.

Trent's head wrenched backward. His pistol fell to the ground; his body stiffened. He took a few steps back toward Kelly and fell over her. Kelly slammed her head into his face and spun around. She contorted her body and squirmed until she was next to Trent. With her hands behind her back, she pushed backward into his side and pulled the knife from his belt. Within seconds, she began cutting her ties. Trent struggled on the ground, cupping his hands on the side of his head. He managed to stand. He looked down at Kelly and delivered a kick to her face. She collapsed.

Pierce grabbed the table and slid it at Trent with all his might. The laptops crashed onto the floor, cutting off the high-pitched sound. The table smashed Trent's thighs with enough force to send him a step backward. Pierce lurched forward and fell onto his side, struggling with his legs to break the zip ties around them. Only feet from the pistol, he squirmed forward and managed to get a hand on the gun.

Trent shook his head. He swung around to see Pierce aiming the weapon at him and immediately withdrew Kelly's pistol from the back of his waistband. Pierce pulled the trigger in rapid succession; the hangar erupted in thunderous gunshots. Trent leapt to the side and returned fire. Pierce felt a thousand-pound weight hit him in the chest and burning pain in his left shoulder.

He was sure he'd hit Trent somewhere near the collar bone at least once. He continued to fire as Trent made it to the front of the plane. The plane's engine sputtered to life. Pierce shot at the tires. One went flat.

Pierce pulled the trigger again, nothing happened. He turned the gun to see that the slide was locked to the rear.

Empty. He was bleeding. He had a tiny hole in the meat of his shoulder that blazed like a red-hot poker had been jammed into it.

Trent darted in front of the plane and rushed back to Kelly, who was still a pile on the floor.

He sneered at Pierce. "Fifteen rounds. You're out."

He ripped a long plastic zip tie from his waistband and fed it into itself, making a loop. He slipped the loop around Kelly's neck.

Pierce struggled against the zip ties on his legs. The couple behind him were now on their sides; he hadn't noticed them screaming until now. He maneuvered his way to Kelly.

Trent jerked the zip tie tight around Kelly's neck and let go. Her head fell back to the floor of the hangar. Her mouth hung open, trying desperately to breathe; her chest heaved under her body armor. Her fingers clawed at the zip tie strangling her.

"Come after me or save her. Your choice," Trent yelled over the plane's engine.

Trent raced back to the front of the plane and climbed into the cockpit. The engine roared as Pierce wormed his way to Kelly, propelling himself across the slick hangar floor with his hands. He grabbed the knife, still on his knees, and cut the zip ties from her neck and legs. She was still breathing.

The plane thundered out of the hangar, sending a blast of wind that whipped Kelly's hair across her face. Trent made it to the runway, but it was pitch black. Pierce couldn't see the plane. No lights.

He cut the ties from his legs and hauled Kelly into his lap. Blood spilled from her mouth, drawing a line down her cheek and onto Pierce's pants.

"Please God, wake up!"

His eyes burned. He slapped her once and those green eyes opened, looking up into his.

Kelly spit out a bit of blood, blinked her eyes, and asked, "Where is he?"

Pierce could barely contain himself. She was okay.

"He's in the plane. How are you?"

"I'm okay."

He helped Kelly to her feet as she looked at him, confused. "What was that sound?"

"Three thousand hertz. I gambled that he had a brain injury from a bullet wound—scar on his head. It's called hyperacusis: high-pitched sounds can cause seizures. The runway is dark. He will probably try to take off without any lights. He's definitely got some backup plan in place to post this video."

In the distance, the plane's engine roared.

CHAPTER 35
PRAGUE, CZECH REPUBLIC

Aphid struggled to understand why this woman was in the air in front of him. Before he could bring himself back to reality, she crashed into him with an impact that sent him flying backward to the floor, knocking the air from his lungs.

The gunshots echoed off the walls as he tried to push the woman off of him. The men had stopped shooting when Deidra had gotten too close to Aphid.

Aphid pushed her face toward the ceiling, and there, on top of him, was this dark-skinned succubus who was responsible for every ounce of pain he'd experienced in his life.

Deidra struggled against his grip; Aphid regretted not working out more often. He would have been able to snap this little bitch in half a few years ago. Her chest had two holes in it, and her left arm no longer worked. She didn't seem to notice or even feel the pain. A cutting chill sliced through Aphid as the woman broke her face free of his grip and looked him in the eye with the coolness of a machine.

His men came into view and grabbed the woman by both arms. Even bleeding to death and staring him in the face, Deidra continued kicking him in the groin and legs as she was ripped off of him and into the air. The men thrust her back into her seat. Aphid stared at the ceiling for a second and caught his breath. His plan would continue. No force on Earth could stop it.

He opened his mouth. His jaw was slightly dislocated. His ribs ached, and he estimated at least two were broken. The men stood over him with extended hands. Silent.

Aphid sat upright and let his men lift him back into his chair.

Again, Deidra stood and grabbed the still-warm teapot from the floor and reeled it back, aiming for Aphid's head. Her face revealed nothing. No expression. It was eerie and terrifying. Before she could launch the teapot, she crumpled to the floor, struggling to breathe.

Aphid casually motioned for his men to place Deidra back in her chair.

They complied. She was wrestling with consciousness; her eyes fluttered, and her head tilted skyward as she struggled to breathe. He leaned toward her, holding his jaw, his other hand clutching his rib cage.

"You're dying now. I sincerely wanted you to witness everything."

Every breath the woman took was shallower than the last.

Tension pneumothorax.

Aphid stood and walked to the window. A long trail of thick, black smoke drew his attention down to a bright, burning building in the distance. His warehouse, just a kilometer away, set ablaze in a flash of light. Dark figures emerged from the building, collapsing onto the dirt and grass-covered ground surrounding his compound. What looked like a hundred police cars circled the bright, burning mass. His men were being executed.

His hands clenched as a muffled series of thuds interrupted the stillness behind him in the room.

He spun to face Deidra. Her eyes were closed. The door was ajar, and both of his men lay slumped on the floor. A black-gloved hand appeared around the door frame and he recognized the familiar shape of a flash-bang grenade flying at him. His world turned white with a sharp, ringing silence.

CHAPTER 36
NAPA, CALIFORNIA

“Can you walk?” Pierce asked.

“I’m good. All good. Just a chipped tooth and cut lip.” Kelly spat a glob of blood onto the concrete. Relieved, Pierce’s body relaxed.

“Good. Go get your rifle off the wall there. Meet me on the tarmac.” Pierce ran ahead into the darkness while Kelly retrieved her rifle from the shelf where Trent had stashed it. She followed close behind, holding her rifle at the ready.

Pierce lay prone onto the tarmac. Kelly approached in a crouch as he worked with his comms radio.

“Are you bleeding?” Kelly asked as she knelt beside him.

“Yes, ma’am. It’s okay. Nothing arterial.”

Kelly laid on her stomach and handed him her rifle.

“How are you going to make this shot in the dark?”

Pierce continued typing on the radio, the green screen illuminating his face. “I’m not. He’s probably going to have to repair that tire, and the lights will be on for that.”

The plane was well over forty yards away from them at the foot of the runway. “Are you going to hack it or something?”

“No. This airport has Pilot-Controlled Lighting. If someone’s coming in for a landing at night, they can use the plane’s radio to turn on the lights of the airport. Almost all private airports have it. It’s so the lights aren’t on all night. If you key your microphone seven times within five seconds, it will turn the lights on for a little while so you can land. This airport is on 188.7 megahertz. When I say go, hit the transmit button seven times.”

“That’s badass,”

Pierce brought himself to a kneeling position and pulled the M4 rifle to his shoulder. “I can see the shadow of the plane.”

Kelly punched the keys 188.700 into the radio and hit 'enter.' "Ready when you are."

Pierce kept his eye on the scope. "Do it."

Kelly clicked the button seven times in quick succession. A second later, bright white light exploded onto the runway.

"Holy shit. It worked!" Kelly exclaimed, blinking to adjust to the brightness.

Pierce readied the scope on the plane. His hands were freezing. "Got him. The lights scared him. He's getting back into the plane."

He flipped off the safety; Kelly covered her ears.

He stood and began shooting—advancing on the plane. Thunder erupted from the barrel. Kelly watched as Pierce calmly sent all thirty rounds in the magazine into the plane's cockpit. In less than two seconds, he loaded a new magazine. He continued firing single shots into the aircraft until the second magazine was empty again. He loaded a third magazine and continued his advance on the plane in silence.

The plane's engine slowed, coughing and sputtering in intermittent bursts of life with the silence following the gunfire.

Pierce twisted around to Kelly. "Go back and secure the laptops."

Kelly yelled something into the night air. Pierce couldn't make it out, but he recognized it as Tradecraft. In an instant, the searing pain in his shoulder disappeared and a rush of energy swept through him. The plane's engine sputtered two final coughs of life and died.

Pierce sprinted the twenty yards with rifle in hand, keeping the barrel leveled steadily on the plane. He approached from the rear. It was almost silent. Sounds of liquid pouring out of the plane onto the tarmac permeated the night.

He saw Trent slumped onto the window and readied the rifle. He held the weapon steady at Trent's head, opened the rear door of the plane, and reached around the headrest. He placed his hand onto the side of Trent's neck.

No pulse.

After a search of the plane, Pierce pulled three laptops and two cell phones from a duffel bag. He searched for more electronic devices but found none. He threw them all into the duffel and zipped it up. He retrieved a plastic emergency kit from behind the rear of the plane and tossed it onto the seat. He flipped it open and withdrew a bright orange flare gun and fired a single flare into the footwell of the front seat.

The small blaze blossomed into an inferno, catching onto the growing pool of fuel pouring from the plane's wings. Flashes of heat lapped at his back as he turned to the hangar. He launched into a full speed sprint back to Kelly and the two civilians.

Kelly had removed the zip ties and duct tape from David Morris and his wife. The three of them stood hunched over the computers on the table as Pierce ran into the hangar. Kelly met Pierce's gaze with an expressionless stare.

"The video uploaded."

CHAPTER 37

NAPA, CALIFORNIA

Pierce darted around the table. A blue rectangle sat in the middle of the screen flashing *File Uploaded.*

Kelly faced Pierce. "What do we do?"

Pierce eyed David Morris. "Where did it upload?"

"It's in our server. All my posts have to get run through our public relations office before they post officially. They are probably screening it now."

"Call them. *Now!*"

Morris snatched the phone from the table and fumbled through his list of contacts. He tapped it and put the phone on speaker.

It rang—and continued ringing.

Pierce shook his head. "If your people are alive, they're about to post a video they think is harmless. It has the potential to kill about ninety million people if it is what we think it is. There's a good chance they're dead. Shut your site down now," Pierce ordered.

"My site? The entire site? I don't have the ability to just pull it offline."

"You have thirty seconds to shut the site down before I get angry, David."

David paused, his face sweating. He stared at the ground in thought with a hand in his hair, shaking his head. He pulled his cellphone back out of his pocket and dialed another number. Within seconds, a voice answered.

"Shut the site down. It's David. ...Yes, the whole fucking site. Shut it down now! Password: Viking Saturn 1176." David continued to stare at the floor as he listened.

Kelly stood behind him, helping his wife stand. After an elongated minute, David looked from Kelly to Pierce.

"It's done. They put it into maintenance—no one will be able to access anything online. Do you know how long it needs to be offline? I'm losing, like, a million dollars an hour here."

Kelly spoke, surprising Pierce. "It's going to be offline until we say otherwise. I'll redirect the team to your facility in Silicon Valley. Is that where the file would be?"

"Yes. It's in the server. Once something posts online, it transfers to our servers in Tennessee. It's isolated here for now."

"For every dollar you lose in the next few days, it's about a thousand lives you *saved*."

Pierce wiped his mouth in exhaustion. Police lights emerged on the dark road beside the airport. He and Kelly exchanged glances and pulled the FBI windbreakers from their side pockets.

As he threw on the windbreaker, Pierce said to David and his wife, "You did the right thing. Are you both alright?"

CHAPTER 38
PRAGUE, CZECH REPUBLIC

"Madam?"

A local paramedic knelt over Deidra. Searing pain tore into her side. As her eyes opened, she noticed the site of the pain. A small plastic tube protruded from her side. Her shirt had been ripped off; her breasts covered by a hotel towel. Two pieces of plastic tape covered the small, dark bullet holes in her chest. Blood had formed around them in caked rectangles. She was still in the hotel room.

"*Byl jsi zastřelen. Museli jsme vložit trubici do vaší hrudi.*"

Deidra didn't understand him.

"*Anglicky prosím*," Deidra replied. English, please.

"Ah. Yes. Sorry. You are okay. You were shot in chest. You need hospital. We had to put tube in your chest for you to breathe."

She strained to lift her head.

"Please madam. We will get you to hospital. I see your identification and you are State Department for USA, yes?"

She nodded and glanced at the young paramedic. She seized the edge of his reflective vest.

"What happened out there?" She motioned out the window.

The young man's face fell.

"The building was set on fire very fast. They rescued several of your Americans from there. No one else survived. They also rescued a woman there who works with you at State Department.

Deidra's entire body unwound. She nodded, relieved Jennifer was okay.

"Hospital."

CHAPTER 39
PRAGUE, CZECH REPUBLIC

*****THREE HOURS EARLIER*****

Jennifer Goram left the hotel with her security man to check the area police stations while Deidra stayed to launch the drone.

They climbed into the back of a taxi, and Jennifer told him to take them to the nearest police station.

Jennifer's phone vibrated in her pocket.

HIG.

"Yes?"

"Ma'am, we found the building. It's a warehouse just north of the Praha Rugby Club. Only a few miles from where you are. I–I can't reach the Director. We've been calling her phone and the secure line."

"Can you turn on the microphone on the laptop?"

"We have. We could hear a disturbance, and what sounded like a stun gun or a taser. The laptop shut off after that. I'm not sure what to make—"

"Get the info out to all the local police about the building. I'll do what I can here. Bypass whoever you need to. I don't give a shit."

After the brief ride, they leapt from the taxi. Jennifer read the small sign above the police office door.

'OŘ Praha III - Místní oddělení policie Vysočany'

The cool Prague air carried a hint of diesel. Jennifer eyed the meager building. She was about to break the highest HIG protocol.

Outside the police station, gray painted bricks with a blue stripe lining the top identified the small portion of the building occupied by the police. The windows were barred. Two gray police vehicles sat out front.

Her security guard waited outside while she entered the station.

A man in a police uniform sat behind an open glass window. Jennifer had spent almost a year translating many of the HIG emergency phrases to Czech for HIG operatives stationed in the region. Today, she was grateful for that.

She spoke *Phrase Three* to the man in perfect Czech.

His eyelids drooped and his once taut shoulders slumped.

She continued in Czech, "I'd like to speak to the senior officer here . . . *that's completely okay to get him now.*"

The man nodded and spoke into his radio, "*Pane, okamžitě přijďte ke stolu.*" *Sir, please come to the desk immediately.*

"Thank you," Jennifer said. "It's completely fine."

Another police officer came around the corner. He squinted at the scene before him.

"What's this? What is going—"

Jennifer snapped her fingers at the man to refocus his attention and shouted the Phrase again. The man's outstretched hand motioning to his desk officer slowly fell back to his side, his face relaxed.

"Now, I need you both to do something to save the day and make yourself heroes. You *are* heroes, correct?"

They nodded. The desk officer much more lethargic, having been exposed to the Phrase a second time.

"Great. You can accept everything here because you know it all to be true. Captives are being held in a warehouse. Your men, *all* of the men, you will call throughout Prague. Every team and every unit will converge on this building. You will call the entire police force. Terrorists are holding trafficked captives in this building. The terrorists need to be killed. Don't you agree?" The men nodded. "You can easily order them to set the building on fire, use explosives, whatever you like. Get the captives out, storm the building, level it to the ground."

The officers nodded. Their eyes widened in anticipation of the massive operation they were about to conduct.

"Get captives out. Destroy the building. The building is an abandoned warehouse just north of the Praha Rugby Club. Large abandoned warehouse. Say it back to me, please."

"Just north of Rugby Club in Praha. Abandoned warehouse. Rescue victims, save them. Destroy building completely—*all* police."

"Perfect. You will send the best men you have to rescue one more person immediately in the Clarion Congress Hotel, room 727. Do not hesitate. Room 727. Room 727. Now.

"You are both heroes. Thank you. You will notice how excited and determined you feel, and that feeling grows stronger with every breath you're taking now. Building to the true crisis you know you were born to stop."

The men's jaws clenched in unison.

She turned to the door, speaking one last phrase. "You're fully in control, wide awake, it begins...NOW!"

As she exited, she heard immediate shuffling, radio calls, and the man at the desk scrambling with the phone.

The door swung open to an empty sidewalk. Her security man had vanished. Her pulse quickened, sensing someone watching her from some hidden location. She walked to her right toward the towering O2 arena, her steps brisk.

Tires screeched to her left. A small sedan appeared, covered in rideshare stickers. An overweight man leaned from the window extending a yellow device Jennifer couldn't make out. Before she could speak a word, a sharp series of clicks erupted from the device. Her body lost all control. Her teeth slammed shut as every muscle tightened into wood.

In a haze, she felt strong hands snatch her upward. Her body now rested across soft, comfortable material. She tried to force herself back into consciousness, and mentally prepared to use Tradecraft on whomever this man was. Her hair was whipped away from her face, and in an instant, something sharp pinched in her neck. The car shifted as the man plopped into the driver's seat in front of her. A moment later, she heard him speaking in English.

"Sir? It's Pavel. I have her here. I am coming now, only two minutes away. Yes sir. She's fine–asleep."

Fog flooded her awareness, and then, nothing.

CHAPTER 40

NAPA, CALIFORNIA

Pierce retrieved his FBI credentials from the underside of his body armor, handing them to the County Sheriff.

"I didn't know FBI was involved in anything here tonight."

"Trust me, we didn't either."

Kelly rounded the corner of the hangar with David Morris and his wife wrapped in blankets. Two police officers trailed them from the hangar.

David Morris walked straight to Pierce and extended his hand. "I... I don't know what to say."

Pierce shook his hand. "You and me both. You guys please get some rest. Here's my card if you need anything."

Pierce handed him a white card with only a number on it.

David Morris placed a hand on Pierce's shoulder and leaned closer to him. "I'll be in touch. I think I know who you guys are and I might be able to help."

The couple walked off to the ambulance with the officers and Kelly set a course toward Pierce. His eyes widened, eyebrows darting upward. She still looked full of life. Her cheeks were flush, and her eyes were bright and vibrant with color. She walked with her confident, unmistakable stride. Her presence gave him a renewed faith in the world he couldn't quite place.

Kelly began undoing her body armor as she neared him. "What's on your mind?"

"What do you know about furniture?" Pierce asked.

Kelly glanced back, confused.

"I need to seriously redecorate my house."

Kelly's eyes lit up. "Then I guess we've got shopping to do."

Pierce wrapped his arm around her and pulled her into him. She tucked her head into his shoulder and he cupped her head. “Let’s get you to a dentist first.”

Her soft voice was muffled by his shirt. “Deal.”

CHAPTER 41

YORKTOWN, VIRGINIA

Pierce steered his old Jaguar into the gravel driveway of HIG. He kept the windows down, enjoying the warm morning air of Yorktown.

He put the car in park under the covered entrance and took a moment to re-center. He hadn't been inside since Alex had been killed. He removed his aviator sunglasses and slipped them into the pocket of his white shirt.

Jennifer stood waiting in the doorway. Having been made the acting director of HIG, she had pulled all the stops to ensure the video, and any system that it had touched, were destroyed.

"Hey, handsome." Her face was sympathetic and soft.

Pierce hugged her. They stood in silence, sharing everything without a word.

"Come on in," Jennifer said. "Deidra should be out of the hospital today. Won't be back on the job until next week."

They wandered into the kitchen, and Jennifer handed Pierce a cup of coffee. An oil painting of Alex hung on the wall where the Mary Celeste ship had been. Pierce stood in silence and admired the portrait of his mentor.

"I've never met a better man," Pierce said, taking in a breath.

"Nor have I."

Jennifer took a sip of coffee and slid a small, padded manila envelope across the granite counter. Pierce picked it up.

"This it?"

"Yep. He's downstairs waiting for you. In the aquarium. We got all the intel we need."

"Thanks, Jennifer. For everything."

Jennifer nodded. "See you in a bit."

Pierce strode past the kitchen to a steel door painted to look like wood. He punched a nine-digit code into a keypad nestled in the rock wall and the door unlocked with a sharp click. He descended a set of metal stairs to the main operations center of HIG. To his immediate left, another locked door clicked open after he entered a second code. He went down another flight of metal stairs into a dimly lit, long, gray hallway. He passed the several doors leading to storage rooms, sleeping quarters, and offices. At the end of the hallway, a security officer armed with a submachine gun stood next to a heavy, green door.

"Mr. Reston."

"Hey, Mike."

"He's waiting for you."

The guard moved aside and typed a code into a keypad in the wall. The green door slid open to a dimly lit room.

In the center of the room sat a ten-foot, squared prison cell made of two-inch-thick Lexan, the plastic used to make airplane windshields. HIG operators referred to it as 'the aquarium.' The smell of rubbing alcohol lingered in the air.

White lights flickered to life above the aquarium. There, inside the glass box, crumpled sideways on a mattress, was the man who'd orchestrated Alex's murder. Aphid's frame was thinner than Pierce imagined. Dressed in a white jumpsuit, he rose to sit upright and eyed the door, straining to see past the light into the dark room. Pierce walked into the light and approached the narrow, rectangular hole in the glass used to deliver food. A white chair sat on either side of the slight opening. Pierce sat and stared at Aphid through the glass.

"Mister Pierce Reston, I assume?" Aphid's voice echoed through the small opening.

Pierce leaned down and flicked on the microphone system, allowing their voices to come across the speakers on either side of the transparent wall of the cube. "You're correct. I hear you like to be called Aphid. Is this how I should address you?"

"If you please."

Aphid stood from his bed and stretched. He hadn't shaved in a couple of days. "You'll have to excuse my appearance. I've not been able to choose my own outfits in here. I assume you're turning me over to the government soon?" Aphid stalked to the white chair and took a seat.

"I'm not sure that's in the cards for you, my friend."

Aphid's jaw tensed. "Oh?"

"Probably not. We like to keep things in-house here."

"I'll assume that my stay here won't be very comfortable."

Pierce assessed the man behind the glass.

"When our team removed your video from the servers in San Jose, I finally figured out why we had so many missing marketing experts across America. The video you made would have killed anyone who was in the more suggestible range of the spectrum. If your plan worked, you'd have killed more people than a dozen nuclear weapons combined."

Aphid stared back at Pierce in defiant silence.

"I think you actually did a great job on the script. You could have worked for us here at HIG," Pierce said.

"*You* are the ones who made it necessary."

"Well, I guess we all have our opinions. I have a printout of the script from your video here. I think it was pretty well written. I'm gonna to read it to you."

Aphid's eyes widened. His body stiffened in the chair.

Pierce reached in his pocket and pulled out the manila envelope he'd gotten from Jennifer. "Our men found something in your briefcase I think you'll want back. It looks important. I wanted to make sure you have it back."

He tore open the envelope and slowly withdrew the item. Aphid's face froze in horror. The long, silver letter opener glistened in the light as Pierce pushed it through the slit and closed the narrow door, preventing Aphid from disposing of it.

Pierce pulled out a green piece of paper with typed words on it and cleared his throat.

"Aphid, listen. Going *down* to *up*hold the reasons we dislike ourselves..."

He continued shouting the sequence despite Aphid holding his hands over his ears. It did no good. Pierce wove the words into Aphid's mind through the loudspeaker.

Aphid, dazed, stumbled back to the chair and slumped into it. His eyes searched the room and settled with softness and desire on the silver letter opener.

“Enjoy your day.” Pierce strolled to the exit. As he left, the metallic scrape of the letter opener being lifted off the concrete floor echoed in the silence.

The door snapped closed behind him.

PHRASE SEVEN

ACKNOWLEDGEMENTS

My sincerest thanks:

Foremost, to my editor-in-chief, Deserae Hunter. She did more teaching than editing, and Deserae did a ***lot*** of editing. During our time editing this book, she accused me of overusing the words 'pull' and 'look.' I disagreed until she highlighted them all and the book became a sea of yellow. Thank you for your patience. Her surgical editing skills, and hours spent trudging through my first work of fiction, all came together to tell this story of 'fiction' to the worlddd. (Typo left just for her.)

To Sara, who's kept the entire project (me) on track throughout disruptive setbacks and pitfalls. Her facial expressions as I'd hand her new pages of the book after they were written were priceless and made me want to keep writing.

My children were key in all of this. During a worldwide crisis, they kept their chins up, and helped dad stay focused during 'writing time.'

To my parents and sister, who've not only served as a guidepost in my life, but as the inspiration to do great things, and try anything.

My sincere thanks to the manager of Hotel Carlo IV. When I said, "I need to get onto the roof of the hotel because I'm writing about a naked woman up there," he responded, "Tell me more..."

My thanks to Margarita Videvik, who assisted me in ensuring every detail of Prague was accurate and offered to 'FaceTime' me through all of the chase scene areas before my trip.

To Pavl, my driver in Prague. The driver in the book was named Pavel *before* my trip. When I got into the car and he introduced himself, I got scared for a second. His patience in driving me around for days visiting abandoned warehouses and random places in the woods didn't go unnoticed.

I'm deeply grateful to the staff of the Prague Hotel Clarion Congress and the hotel manager, Svetlana. I asked to speak to the manager and after telling her I needed to observe an abandoned warehouse and launch a drone out of a high up window, she patiently walked me from room to room until I found the right angle.

To the staff and owner of Yorktown Pub. I wrote many scenes sitting in here, and they tolerated my incessant weird questions, such as, "What's the average occupancy at around 8:50 PM?" and "What's the meaning of that painting of the guy on the wall?"

I'd have not written this book without watching Dan Brown's masterclass on writing. Learning the craft of fiction is the hardest endeavor I've ever undertaken, and Dan made it approachable. Dan's books inspired my drive to ensure every detail was accurate, down to which lever in the Café Mozart men's bathroom would open a window, and which one didn't work.

Acknowledgments

ABOUT THE AUTHOR

Chase Hughes is the bestselling author in the world, according to his mom.

Chase is the CEO of Applied Behavior Research. After 20 years in the US Military, Chase is a leading expert in behavior profiling, influence, and interrogation. He teaches the most elite government and business teams in the world and is the author of the #1 bestselling book on persuasion, people-reading, and influence, *The Ellipsis Manual*.

Chase also works around the world as a trial consultant, teaching jury selection, cross-examination, and critical influence and behavior skills to law firms.

His courses bring powerful techniques designed for intelligence work to civilians and companies.

Applied Behavior Research is based upon a single vision, 'We rise by lifting others.' Chase now resides in Virginia Beach, Virginia with his family.

Chase can be contacted at www.chasehughes.com

CONTINUE READING FOR AN EXCERPT FROM THE NEXT BOOK IN THE HIG SERIES, 'BELGRADE ARCHER'.

CHAPTER 1

NORFOLK, VIRGINIA

"Sir, we need you to see this. Something in the water." Captain Brad Cooper had only taken command of his ship, a Guided Missile Destroyer, three months ago. Now tied to the Pier, an urgent call about something in the water was unexpected.

He made his way to the quarterdeck where two men stood watch in their dress uniforms.

"Chief? What's going on?" the Captain asked.

"Sir, there's something in the water here, and it looks like a big ol' boat turned upside down."

"Why is this urgent? It's six in the morning."

"Sir, it..has antennas coming out of the *bottom* of it—like big ones."

Without a word, Brad whirled and raced up several sets of stairs to the bridge. As the high-up control center of the ship, there were giant, steel binoculars mounted to the deck to allow the lookouts to identify far-away ships while they were out to sea. The Captain rounded the corner, almost out of breath, the speed at which he ran made him grateful he was in his morning workout clothes. He stepped up to the platform and swiveled large, mounted binoculars, referred to as 'Big Eyes,' toward the floating object. It was only a hundred yards from an Aircraft Carrier in the next dock. The cool spring breeze whipped across the decks.

He paused, allowing his eyes to adjust. It *did* look like a huge, upturned boat, but he knew it wasn't. Tall antennas coming from the object reached skyward. He leveled the binoculars on the front of the black, floating object and his breathing caught. The blood rushed from his face.

"Jesus Christ."

He swallowed hard, pulled away from the binoculars, and blinked to refocus his vision. He leveled his eyes into the binoculars once more and saw it just below the water's surface. A Russian Naval emblem.

Not an upturned boat. The top of a gargantuan Russian Nuclear Submarine, adrift in the harbor.

Captain Cooper leapt from the platform and shot into the bridge. He grabbed the ship's loudspeaker and announced a full Security Alert across the ship. The alarm blared through the speakers and echoed off the nearby ships in the harbor.

He called the Chief on watch at the Quarterdeck and instructed him to notify all the nearby ships on the secure radio.

The Captain ran back to the Big Eyes and steadied them again on the submarine. The uppermost hatch was laid open, and the sub tilted at the mercy of the wind.

There's either no one inside, or we're about to be at war.